THE NUN

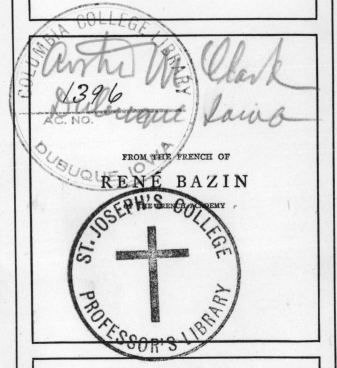

THE NUN

(L'ISOLÉE)

FROM THE FRENCH OF

RENÉ BAZIN

OF THE FRENCH ACADEMY

NEW YORK
CHARLES SCRIBNER'S SONS
1908

Published March, 1908

Contents

I.

II.

III.

IV.

V.

THE NUN.

I.

THE EVENING IN JUNE.

"SISTER PASCALE, your eyes are red."

"Not that I've been crying. There's a chill in the wind to-night."

"Yes, and there was hard work in the school to-day. You will be killing yourself, Sister Pascale."

A young, unsteady voice, with gaps in it caused by physical fatigue, replied:

"They are such darlings, my little girls; and yet, in a week, not one of them would think of me again—nor, perhaps, would any one in the wide world." And the speaker laughed.

A murmur of words, hardly articulate, obviously often rehearsed, seemed to surround and envelop the young Sister with their tenderness. "Child! when will you be rational? You are trying to get us to say how much we care for you."

"Who would think this baby was twenty-three to-day?"

"Yes, this very day, the 16th of June, 1902."

"There, you see, we know all about your age!"

A pleasure in merely being together, in being quiet, in loving one another apart, visited all these hearts. And she who was in authority, raising her eyes beyond the enclosing courtyard, and beyond the sky-line of distant houses, said:

"It is good to breathe. People are fond of libelling the air of our smoky Lyons, but it does really smell of the country; don't you think it does?"

In a few moments' silence, all eyes were lifted; the sick or weary breast breathed in that joy of summer which the city had not quite absorbed or destroyed. These souls, inspired to worship and to the giving of thanks on behalf of the world, offered their gratitude in silence.

They were five women—five nuns, dressed in blue homespun, white frontlet, and black veil, within the enclosure of a school, where an alley, paved with cement and sheltered by a roof, ran the whole length of the playground. They kept for the use of their own "Community" this narrow retreat, and their habit was to gather there in their free time, when, as now, the school-children were gone. They felt more intimate there and also better screened from the curious eyes of neighbours; for the left wing of the house, towards the east, was nearly surrounded by buildings. Five women: and one only was not young. She was called Sister Justine, and had held office as Superior for five-and-twenty years: a woman built for action, square, broad-hipped, with a

large face, a kind, round nose, a skin paled by
habitual privation of fresh air, eyes brown and
full of cheerful life, eyelids that could open or close
indeed, but knew no other trick, and had never
given a subtle expression or a shade of meaning
to any glance of hers. A white hair or two
sprouted on her upper lip and on her chin: her
few wrinkles were deep within her flesh; a silver
lock of hair, now and then escaping from a frontlet
carelessly put on, showed her to be aged about
sixty years.

Had Sister Justine remained in her native
place with her parents, working people of Colmar,
she would have become what the peasants call
a "godmother," a housewife dominant in her own
home, and, not seldom, in a neighbour's; a man-
aging woman, somewhat feared, but always benef-
icent. But at twenty she had entered the
congregation of St. Hildegarde, which has its
Mother-House at Clermont-Ferrand, and since
then had returned once only to Alsace, on the eve
of the war of 1870. In her was evident the war-
like and frontier-guarding blood of her race.
Quick in decision, brief in speech, never rescinding
an order, clear in intelligence, ready in reply, more
courageous than the average of men, she had
never ceased to be the counsellor and the support
of a throng that constantly shifted and changed
about her. Children, parents, the random poor,
with weaknesses, grievances, and sufferings of
many kinds—very secret as well as very common
—had confidence in her strength, well aware of
her tenderness for those obscure and insignificant

ones of the social world who recognised in her one of themselves, yet a representative whose dignity they shared. When they were at a loss for the thing to be done, they were wont to say, "Let's go to Sister Justine."

And they found her always ready to set out, far more intent upon the remedy than curious about the evil, never dismayed, and never uselessly given over to emotion. In her gown of homespun blue, of which the sleeves were generally turned back, like those of a field-worker, in her white frontlet and black veil, she would have travelled round the world with a good will. But her journey was the daily circle of the classes in her school and of some poor houses in its neighbourhood. She gave the lessons to the tall girls, those who were in their last school year. Among the nuns also she was the adviser, the prop, the shelter. In the town she was summoned hither and thither by those who did not so much as know her. Her name was called upon in place of the name of Providence, which was not invoked. And in this rough work she did not wear out, so calm was she as well as alert, going, going, on her strong, short legs. "Never to belong to yourself," said she; "that is the way never to be tired."

After Sister Justine the eldest of the Sisters was not yet forty years old; and those who saw her at a distance, or had a brief view of her, thought her much younger. Slender and tall, almost unwrinkled, her eyes often cast down, her lips delicate and almost blue, so pale they were, she bore something in her face and in her attitude that was haughty, virginal, and austere. She resembled, with the addition of reality and life, a woman-martyr figured in a stained-glass window, rigid, upright, with one hand upon a sword, symbol of her strength, of her death, and of her honour. When she turned those eyes upon another—even if this were a child—the impression was not softened. The eyes of Sister Danielle, exceedingly dark under lovely eyebrows, expressed a soul full of self-diffidence, closely curbed, and so exacting towards itself that is was thought to be exacting towards others. But this woman had tamed herself; she went in fear, despite her blameless experience; she was a wise virgin anxiously watching for any wind that might breathe upon her lamp.

Almost tragic of aspect, she bore the traces of the cost at which certain spirits overcome nature by will. She had an ardent heart; and its enthusiasm now was manifest only in the eagerness of duty. Those who watched her knew her to be capable of heroism, and sensitively bent on keeping that capacity secret. To her the Superior had entrusted the second class and the accounts of the Community; but she might have been charged with the cooking, or the washing, or another task of any kind. She was chosen to accompany Sister Justine when a ceremonial visit had to be paid to the Cardinal Archbishop of Lyons, or to the Abbé Le Suet, "Monsieur le Supérieur" of the Order. And as all she did was done with scrupulous exactitude, Sister Danielle did not escape the sisterly admiration of the observant

and tender witnesses in whose company she lived.
She too watched, but her care was that she should
not be too dearly loved for fear of the love of self
that might ensue. Nor even in intimate inter-
course, in conversation on summer evenings, in the
courtyard and the playground, did she relax her
reserve; she asked few questions, she smiled little.

When she was alone—that is, when she was at
prayer—this close spirit was unlocked, and the
fire therein took flight in flame, went up to God.
Danielle then let loose her love upon things visible
and invisible, upon the children of her religious
adoption, upon the miseries she knew and those
she knew not, in tears and cries and the clamour
of her prayer. And this was but a child of poor
people, born in a peasant family of day-labourers
in that country of Corrèse, where the chestnut
trees shade the soil from a southern sun. Over
the door of her cell, on the inner side, she had written, *Libenter et fortiter*. The daily recitation of the
Office had taught the Sisters some little Latin.

A peasant also was the little Sister Léonide,
but of another province. She was the child of
the Lyons country side, of the district of Lozanne,
where large villages lift on vine-clad hills their
wide, tiled roofs like a heap of hollow shells. She
had laboured, she had dug, she had reaped, she
had gathered the vintage, putting all the strength
she had into her daily toil; and now she prolonged,
in the religious dress, her lowly and almost entirely
manual labour, keeping the lamps in order, sweeping out the class-rooms, and teaching the alphabet
on Sundays to the little pupils, the very young

children whom the mothers of the district, bent on a country excursion, on the streets, or on a dance, brought to the Sisters of St. Hildegarde for the day. She was short and swarthy, with two red patches on her cheeks—"kisses of the kitchen range," she called them; and although she was not yet thirty, all her teeth were gone. Her disfigured and discoloured lips hardly used any words but these: "Yes, Sister"; "Of course I will, Sister"; "Well, come in, little one"; "Sit down, ma'am, I'll run and tell the Superior." Entirely simple, afraid of nothing, obedient for the sake of love, freely self-forgetful, she might have written over her cell door, *Ecce ancilla Domini*. But she had not thought of it. All Lyons knew her; the tram-conductors—some of them—used to take her by the arm to help her in when she came with her basket full of potatoes and carrots from the market on the Quai Saint Antoine. "Up, little Mother, jump!" they said. She would reply: "Only little Sister, as yet," and they laughed.

The two other nuns came from a far different environment; they were Sister Edwige, born at Blois, daughter of a station-master in the Indre-et-Loire country, and Sister Pascale, daughter of a Lyons silk-weaver. These two were earnest friends. The one concealed her preference by reason of universal charity, the other showed it by reason of weakness. To be near Sister Edwige, to see her, and to hear her, was to be aware of all that is uttered in the word Mercy. The eternal compassion had its abode in her. Kindness without limit, without weariness, without distinction of persons, went forth from her face and from her hands. It was manifest in her grace of movement, in the clear form of her cheek, in her limpid eyes which proffered respect, admiration, devotion, pity—and always love; soft eyes, ignorant of deceit, hatred, or so much as irony; eyes like the eyes of a child to whom had been added the knowledge of sorrow; eyes so lovely, and of a tenderness so chaste and wide, that the Sisters said, "Sister Edwige's eyes give us God."

Hers was the primary class in the school, that of the children six and seven years old. She had the motherhood of a virginal spirit, and others loved her; shy people, discouraged ones, unpromising ones, those who needed special protection— all, having once seen Sister Edwige, sought her. She had very ready and accessible tears. She looked as though she were reaping and gathering love on behalf of the supernal mercy visible in her. One might well have said to her: "Raise your hand over us, and we shall be healed." Many had stammered words of somewhat this meaning. But at once her front was darkened, her rays withdrawn, and the charm that brought her so much love had vanished. She seldom left the house, besides, having plenty of work in the school.

Her personal distinction and her youth, as much as her goodness, had gained her the heart of the youngest of the Sisterhood, Pascale. Like all very intelligent girls born in the labouring classes of French towns, Sister Pascale had a taste

for good manners, an aristocratic sense whereby she
perceived, in the street, in a conversation, in
the design of a piece of decoration—everywhere,
the character of the elegant, of the appropriate,
of the distinctively French. She seldom made mis-
takes, and this critical taste had been entangled
with a great deal of envy in the days before her
entry into the Convent. She had been a pretty
girl in the world—not a beautiful one, but a
pretty one, with partly *cendré*, partly tawny, fair
hair, light eyes with points of lively gold—eyes
that brightened with every word, whether heard
or spoken, a rather short nose, firm, youthful
cheeks that were rounded when she laughed, very
red, fresh and mobile mouth. She was one of
those pale women who have been blooming once,
and would easily bloom again. She had no colour,
and there was always a slight darkness, beneath
her eyes. Her laugh was ready; her figure slender
and flexible. Even under her heavy homespun
Sister Pascale looked as though she loved running
and would have used her pupils' skipping-rope had
there been no one to see. There was much of the
child in her, of the Southern French child, careless
of to-morrow as those are who have kept nothing
of yesterday; and she had been secured from all
peril by the example and traditions of her family,
people as steadfast as the Lyons rocks. The
Convent had not robbed her of her frank utterance,
her vivacity, and her exceeding sensibility. She
could not endure to see blood, nor to dress an
abscess, nor to hear an operation detailed. In
the novitiate her trainers had tried to cure the

little town girl of these absurdities, but without
success. Her pleasures also seemed to them ex-
cessive—her delight in a flower, in the light of a
lovely day, in a sunset, or in a beautiful child.
She much preferred those of her pupils who were
pretty, or who were well dressed, or, at least, better
dressed than the others; and of this fault she was
wont to accuse herself. For frankness dwelt in
this soul which was on the way towards peace, but
did not yet possess it, and perhaps would never
possess it wholly. The Sisterhood loved her for
her youth, for her spirit, for her great sincerity,
and also for her weakness, and for the sake of the
help which, ingenuously and often, this little companion in the sisterly life asked of their graver
years.

The five nuns of St. Hildegarde lived together
in a house noisy by day, silent at night-fall. All
were over-worked. The daily recitation of the
Office after evening school, the meditation and
Mass of every morning, the care of a certain number of pupils who took their mid-day meal within
the Convent, the correction of school exercises,
and then—for the elder ones especially—the innumerable affairs of the poorer quarter of the city
to which they ministered, and in which their goodwill was called upon to excess, to exhaustion—
these things filled all the days, the months, the
years. Throughout this incessant occupation, in
this forgetfulness of self, and in this poverty, they
enjoyed the sweetness, little known outside convent walls, that comes of companionship—albeit
often silent—with elect ones, beings entirely

worthy of love, whose energies are all at the command of charity. They formed a group more closely united than a family; none the less had they gathered from dissimilar places and conditions, and for causes that differed also: Sister Justine urged by her faith and by her love of action; Sister Danielle moved by her zeal for spiritual perfection and drawn by the invisible; Sister Edwige called by her love for the poor; Sister Léonide by her humility; Sister Pascale led by her distrust of herself and by her desire that among saints, and in face of their example, her days might be counted in unassailable security.

There was among them a complete liberty; they heard each other, without surprise, speak according to individual temperament and under the impulse of separate character.

On this evening in June they had returned from the service of Benediction in the Church of Saint Pontique. The apse of the church was but a few steps from their door, on a *place* planted with two rows of plane-trees. When they had looked towards the open east, over the little wall of the playground, as the Superior had done, three of them began their walk up and down the courtyard, Sister Danielle and Sister Léonide flanking the stout Superior.

The other two did not at once leave the sight before their eyes. It was not very beautiful; but Sister Edwige looked, with eyes made tender by admiration, at the lower sky, at the tops of poplars planted along the Rhone and visible between distant houses, and she felt the sweetness which

the sun's farewell imparts to all things for a
moment, penetrating them and rendering them
all glorious and translucent. The other nun,
Pascale, the youngest, turned her head slowly to
watch the fading of the sky-line of houses and the
coming, in the hollows of windows, of lights by
twos and threes, and the vague movement of life
within. On all hands rose the noise of labours
drawing to a close; like the sound of the country,
this city clamour was composed of actions and
cries and calls, of footsteps on the pavements,
voices in the lanes, hammerings growing fewer and
longer between, the scream of a siren giving the
signal of departure on the river, resounding noises
of timber on the wharves—all gradually absorbed
by the prodigious silence settling over the city
and seizing it by increasing and enlarging intervals. Sister Pascale was thinking of things gone
by, and of the children scattered through the city
spaces.

Night came, with its deceptive peace; for
nothing had stopped but labour only: not pain,
nor poverty, nor hatred, nor vice. Only a few
sequestered and victorious spirits had peace.

"Are you feeling the heat of this long day, Sister
Pascale?" asked Sister Edwige. "It was all but
unbearable in my class." And she added, with
a secret thrill of joy: "How gently it comes to
an end!" As she said it, she thought of the end
of her youth or of her life.

"No," replied the other; "I am thinking of my
father, who used to stop his loom at this time of
the evening."

"Poor child! And how long ago did you lose him?"

"Four weeks. He died on the sixteenth of May."

The compassionate voice of Sister Edwige resumed hastily: "Oh, I have not kept count, but I have not forgotten my promise for a single day —not one. I only forgot the date."

Behind them, between them, a well-known voice, more decided than theirs, interrupted: "Come with the others, will you?"

It was Sister Danielle.

Sister Edwige and Sister Pascale with the same movement turned and joined the three in their exercise, walking back to the wall on the right, then turning in their up and down walk so as to face the Superior, Sister Léonide, and Sister Danielle. The way was narrow, and did not allow five to go abreast.

"We are talking," said Sister Justine, "of the answers the children give us. Those who come from the secular schools don't know a word of catechism or of Scripture. And those who come straight from home hardly know more."

"Would you believe it," cried Sister Léonide with a laugh; "A new girl came a fortnight ago into the little ones' class, and this is what she said. I asked her what was the first man's name, and she said 'Adam.' And the first woman's name? 'Ad le.' What did she do? What was her sin? 'Oh, I know, Sister, she sneaked an apple.'"

There were a few smiles, but only the little peasant nun who told the story laughed out, with a laugh that rang across the court-yard and over the wall.

"It is not such a very bad answer," said Sister Justine. "If they blundered only over the name of the first woman, there would not be much harm done. But some are asked who is Christ, and say they don't know—there's harm enough there, and fault enough."

"Whose fault?" asked a serious voice.

Two or three veils turned towards the speaker. It was Sister Danielle. There was no reply, but the name of Christ falling on the pure ground of these hearts, rose again, and was rising higher as they spoke or listened:

"Laetitia Bernier came this morning in a new hat with feathers worth at least——"

Sister Justine, not well versed in the fashions, considered for a moment, and then, remembering a ticket seen in a shop-window, finished her sentence: "Worth at least four francs ninety-five," said she.

"That's not dear for a hat," said Sister Léonide, who knew a little of everything.

"And do you know, Sister Léonide," proceeded Sister Justine, "that Laetitia's cousin, Ursula Magre, is quite well again?"

"Yes, Mother; in fact, I met her yesterday, in Place Bellecour, and she didn't know me."

"She didn't see you?"

"Ah yes, she did. It's not nice in an old pupil. But now she is not at her linen-workshop——"

"She doesn't work there now?"

"No."

"Where is she then?"

"Well, she is not with the Salvation Army either."

Sister Léonide coloured. She often brought back with her, from her tasks in the town, tidings that she did not impart to her companions, unless —as now—she was taken unawares, with an ensuing regret for having talked too much. No one present pressed the point. One or two faces wore a look of pity. But Edwige's face was calm. She lifted to the skies, where the night was now come, her wondering gaze; her lips moved, and she seemed to be praying, with the stars for a rosary.

Sister Pascale, her mobile face full of a tragic indignation, noticed nothing except the refusal of recognition and greeting to little Sister Léonide, her old friend, and exclaimed: "What a shame!"

The Superior turned her eyes on the weaver's daughter.

"Yes," cried Pascale, "a shame. Not to know the good Sister who taught one to read, whom one has seen every day for four or five years—it is a kind of ingratitude I can hardly understand."

"But you will see it very often, little girl."

"Then I shall never get used to it. It has hurt me before. Why when I cross the *place* in the morning, going to church, I pass people I have never seen till then, and they look at me as though they hated me madly."

"That's true enough."

"Men of the town—my town; working people, like my people. And I think, 'Do you know

what I am doing for you, wretches?   I am making
mothers, making wives, making happiness for you,
and yet you don't love me!'"

The stout Superior laughed as she saw, in the
twilight, the impassioned face of Pascale.

"There are so many reasons for ingratitude—
good ones and bad ones."

"Oh! good reasons for ingratitude!"

"Why, yes."

"It is not for ourselves that we are despised,"
said the touching voice of Sister Edwige, "and
that is the sad thing."

As she never spoke save piously and wisely, the
four listened. The Sister stooped to put aside a
ball left on the cement of the playground floor,
and raising again her supple figure, continued with
the tone of conviction that came of her great
sincerity:

"To carry our Christ through the world; not
to let Him die within us; to lift Him up as in a
monstrance—not often; but to let Him shine
through, always, habitually—our one Love."

She had told the story of her own life. She
added in a lower tone:

"The rest is not our business. The rest does
not exist."

For a little while there was no sound in the
playground except the hum of the city, and the
whisper of the felt shoes of the nuns stirring the
dust of the pavement.

"And you, Sister Danielle, what is your ambition?   Sister Edwige has told hers."

The nun thus questioned hesitated, because of

the embarrassment she felt whenever she had to appear, to speak, to arrest the attention of others; then she obeyed:

"I should wish to buy back souls, in secret. It does one so much good, when one is suffering, to think that one is bearing some of the burdens of the over-burdened."

"Well, you'll certainly have your wish," said the loud and laughing voice of the Alsatian; "we have had, and we shall have, trials enough. And you, Sister Léonide?"

"Oh, as for me, whatever you like, so long as I don't have to give orders."

"Why not?"

"Because I shall never be able to do anything but just what I have to do now."

"And you, Sister Pascale? Now, let us see whether she really deserves that we should care for her as we do."

"I am certainly not holy," said the young and unsteady voice; "and I want you all—I always want you, that you may help me to become better. That is my ambition." Sister Pascale looked at them all, one by one, with the warmth of her eyes, which was like the first warmth of morning.

"But I want something besides," she added. "I want our little girls. You know I don't love them all alike—that's the worst of it. But whenever I see one—even one of those I care less about—my heart melts."

"That is true," said Sister Edwige; "they are life growing up, they are divine grace going by."

Their words remained within the narrow group they made as they walked.

Meanwhile, the huge town within which they were lost had ceased to labour. Had they been able to hear and see the life of but a single street, close by their school, what a difference would they have perceived between themselves and "the world"! The men in the work-shop of Japomy the tanner were insulting a foreman, who had given, somewhat too abruptly, a perfectly just order; women, gathered on doorsteps, were slandering the owner and the owner's wife, according to custom. The owner's wife, on her part, was rejecting a husband for her daughter, for the sole reason—sufficient to her mind—that he was of less fortune than the girl; vagrant and ragged applicants were turned rudely away from the doors of employment; wine-shop politicians were fostering their own popularity by preaching hatred of "people who think they are our betters"; some journeymen butchers, rich with their week's wages, were taking an airing in an open carriage; an indigent priest, neglected or forgotten in the hard work of a poor parish, was speaking of his Archbishop with scanty respect. Human pride in many shapes everywhere held sway, fratricidal pride, first sin of man, much older than lust, much older than a lie, much older than the love of gold.

The last pale light of the sky above the courtyard and its two plane-trees was dead. Lights shone in kitchens of multitudes of houses on many levels of the steep city; fog lay over the river; the panting of the last machine in the factories had ceased with the last puff of white steam. Great draughts of air from the plateau of the Dombes disturbed the stifling atmosphere, and spread coolness hither and thither. Two of the Sisters, Edwige and Pascale, folded their arms and hid their hands in their blue sleeves. It was the season and the hour of the flowering of the stars; they clustered so closely that the sand of the playground floor caught minute reflections from their brightness, and the roofs shone faintly. A bell rang within the house and startled Sister Léonide.

"Who can be ringing?" she asked.

"You can see for yourself, my child," said Sister Justine, tranquilly; "go and open the door."

The noise of bolts withdrawn was vaguely audible; then Léonide returned, a little disturbed by the infraction of the rule she had been obliged to commit.

"Mother, it is Ursula Magre, the old school-girl——"

"Yes, I know—why, we were just talking about her. What did she want?"

"She wanted to see you."

"You told her I would see her to-morrow?"

"No, Mother. I told her to come in. There is a hurry about something. She looked—she looked—anyhow."

"Looked what?"

"Funny—no—a good deal put out, with her frizzy head of hair. She is in the parlour, Mother."

The old Superior tapped Sister Léonide twice upon the cheek.

"Think of not being able to keep the door, at your age!"

There was no other reproof. She left the group of nuns who continued their tranquil walk, and the night heard nothing more than four young voices, their quiet speech and their gentle laughter.

Sister Justine threaded the corridor, crossed the house in darkness, and near the front door turned to the left into a small room containing only chairs, where she was accustomed to receive "relations." On the mantelpiece a small petroleum lamp—a glass globe sheltering a little circlet of metal—gave light to the room. And in the unsteady light which the four bare walls reflected, a tall fair-haired girl, upright, her eyelids partly lowered, splendid hair piled on the top of her head, greeted the nun familiarly.

"How do you do, Mother?"

But she did not hold out her hand, nor did she seek a kiss from the old head of the school of her younger days.

"I have something pressing to tell you," continued Ursula, "and I feel it—will you promise to keep it secret?"

"I carry more than my own weight of secrets about with me, my girl—about half the secrets of the district. You can go on. Or shall I help you? Come now, you have not been to see me for five years. You have had a reason. You have made a slip, is that it?"

The tall girl, whose cheeks and short upturned nose and uncovered neck looked rosy and transparent in the lamp light, drew herself up and put

her two hands before her, palms outwards, as
though to keep that matter away; then she said:

"It's not about me, it's about your school.
I've got to tell you that the school is closed."

Sister Justine caught her by the arm, drew her
to the wall, compelled her to sit opposite the little
lamp, took a chair by her.

"What do you mean? Closed? the school?"
She was whiter than her frontlet, and her wrinkles
were suddenly ploughed deep.

"I know it, there's an order for you to leave
your school."

"When?"

"You'll go, you'll have to go, in five or six
days."

"A month before the holidays?"

"So I suppose."

"Oh, my God! And my children, what is to
become of them?"

"That's just it. I thought I would let you
know." The nun bowed herself, bent in two.
Ursula had nothing at her side but a blue and
black bundle from which escaped the cry, "Oh,
my God, my God, how can I bear this?"

Ursula Magre, who was moved by sobs so near
her, had her own lip caught by a slight spasm of
pain. She breathed quickly under her mauve cotton bodice; she glanced awkwardly, now at the old
nun struck down by her news as by a bullet, now
at the light of the lamp beginning to smoke in its
glass globe. Sister Justine sat up, wiped her eyes on
her veil, then taking Ursula's two hands, she said:

"Look here, my child, we must be practical.

We must not run away with our trouble. My whole life is at stake. But you can't be sure; it is just a rumour; we are not obliged to get an authorisation, as the new schools are. Our Mother-House has been authorised——"

The girl made a movement which meant "What do I know about that?"

"The Government said so. We had not to ask permission. The Abbé Le Suet, our Superior, positively read it out."

"I tell you, all the same, that you are to be closed."

"And we have been here forty years. Do you understand? Forty!"

"All the more reason, then."

"And how do you know this?"

Sister Justine let go Ursula's hands. The girl seemed so certain of what she said! The two women looked point-blank at one another, the elder seeking to find out whether she were deceived, the younger angry at the distrust which she read in the Superior's eyes, and none the less angry because she felt a certain degree of shame, albeit in secret, before this old school-mistress who knew so much of her own towns-people that she could read them. Ursula Magre was too proud to confess her embarrassment. She overcame it, and with the audacity she had always shown of old in confessing her own faults, without condescending to ask for their forgiveness, she said:

"It is quite impossible for us to live as you do. I am keeping house, you know—He is a police agent, and it's he who sent me——"

Sister Justine betrayed no surprise. She said in a softened tone:

"Why did he not come instead of you? It is not a pleasant errand."

"Well, it bothers him. He doesn't like business. You know men are afraid, much more afraid than we are. And then———"

"And then?"

"My coming to you from him was to do you a good turn."

"How? Can he prevent this misfortune?"

"He certainly can't."

"Well then?"

Ursula paused a while.

"Listen to me, Mother," she said slowly. "I shouldn't have come at all, if it had been only to make you unhappy. One has no spite against you, one hadn't anything unpleasant in one's school days—and it doesn't follow, even if one isn't pious now-a-days———"

"You never were."

"Even if one has forgotten a lot of things, one's sorry enough to see you put about. That's why. Do you mean to hold out?"

Sister Justine raised her shoulders.

"If I only could! If it were of any use!"

"You mustn't."

"Why?"

"He told me to tell you to give in. It's the law. 'If they make us come—a lot of us,' he said, 'if they make a rumpus,' he said, 'I won't answer for anything. The Mother-House at Clermont-Ferrand may be shut up as well,' he said. 'But if they go quietly of their own accord, for one thing they'll save their Mother-House, and for another thing, Government may allow the nuns, after they have been secularised, to go on teaching. Government will take notice of their good conduct.' That's what he said, Mother."

She waited for a reply. There was none. Sister Justine had at last fully understood that the news was true. She was staring at the wall. Her knees trembled beneath her heavy gown; she saw in thought her nuns going down the three stone steps into the *place*, the children around them in tears, the vacant class-rooms, and the dusty cells. She heard not, but Ursula was saying:

"Well, he says the best thing you could do would be to go out at once—to-morrow, or the day after, without giving notice at all; just quietly. The Mother-House——"

Sister Justine stood up. Her face kept the deep lines of pain that the news had marked there. But now something else was mixed with her grief: the anguish of a decision involving the destruction of her school; the dread of that burden of office which would make her the executioner; the apprehension of that moment, drawing near, when she must tell the dreadful secret to her fond companions now awaiting her, ignorant of all.

"What answer shall I take?" asked Ursula Magre, hesitating. "What are you going to do?"

The nun moved her head. "Be quiet," she said with an effort. "Let me go and tell them."

She crossed the little parlour and took the lamp. She was sobbing, in spite of herself, under the veil she had pulled down. Ursula followed her, wishing that she might give her a kiss for the sake of old times, but she dared not. She went down the steps while the nun, holding up the lamp for her, turned away her poor aged face bathed in tears.

The door was closed. The hand that held the lamp sank down, and Sister Justine, alone, in the shadows of the corridor, in the wind that came warm down the staircase, wept. Her head was bowed, and her tears fell upon the sandy stone worn by the feet of children. She, so strong, so well versed in the art of self-control, was unable to possess herself again. She failed, she leant against the wall. Oh! those Sisters, those dear and innocent fellow-labourers of hers, a few yards away in their peace, in their joy, and she was now to destroy their lives. The sound of a sweet and fresh treble voice—she knew it was the voice of Edwige —reached her from without; she heard it in her agony. Revived by the life that was near, or by a grace sudden and direct, she put the lamp in its place, blew out the flame, and groped her way to the door that opened on the playground.

In the soft and airy night the Sisters were still walking. They took the pleasure of rest from toil and the pleasure of obedience, in their recreation. Nothing had disturbed them; no words, no fading of the beauty of the hour, no slightest apprehension as to the absence of Sister Justine, for they knew poor visitors had much to say. The sounds

of the city were quiet. In the clearer air of night
more distant odours, such as the scent of country
hay, were perceptible. Sister Justine appeared,
her arms extended.

They all moved towards her: "Our Mother,
back again! You have been long away!"

But as they came nearer, notwithstanding the
uncertainty of the light of night, they thought,
they saw, that Sister Justine had the face of one
in grief, and that her open arms were not open
to enfold them, but that they signified the Cross.

"Oh! my girls, my daughters, my little children! our hour of suffering has come!"

She joined her hands, and looking in the face of
Sister Pascale, who was nearest, she said:

"We shall be sent away within a week."

Her four companions came about her, the
smile of welcome hardly yet gone from their lips.
A moment was needed for the sinking of such
news into those hearts. But it reached at last and
explored the inmost capacity of suffering. Loving
much, these women had the more power to suffer.
There were no cries, but shudders, stifled words,
bowed heads, hands that sought each other, eyelids that closed so that they might shut in, if it
were possible, the first of many tears.

Then one voice of distress began:

"O God, have pity on our little girls!"

It was the voice of Danielle.

Sister Edwige said: "Oh, the dear, beloved
house!"

Sister Pascale said: "What will become of *me*
without you all?"

Sister Léonide pulled her nickel watch from her girdle, and walked quickly away. As she moved down the playground, her companions, raising their faces, began to ask questions:

"O Mother, is it possible? They told us we were in order. Is there no appeal? Who told you? Oh, do tell us whether there is any hope at all! Can we do anything? What ought we to do?"

Sister Justine, unmoved outwardly amid their dismay, turned her eyes from the sight of their tears and of their young lips trembling like those of aged women:

"My little children, we must pray hard. It is the one thing, the divine thing. As to human hope—I shall write to-morrow——"

A bell interrupted her with the first of six slow strokes. It was the bell of their rule, and Sister Justine stopped in her phrase. The Sisters walked in single line into the house, the youngest, Pascale, at their head. The "great silence" had set in, not to be broken until eight o'clock of the morning of another day.

*   *   *   *   *   *   *   *   *

Ursula Magre was already far away. She lived, with her protector, near the point of the peninsula of Perrache, between the Saône and the Rhone. She was going to give him an account of her errand. She bit her red lips; she was not grieved, but annoyed, at having had to take a part in this eviction business, and at having to witness at such close quarters the grief of her old

school-mistress. Nothing should make her spend
such another quarter-of-an-hour as that at St.
Hildegarde's. Fargeat might go himself next
time. A man shouldn't make a woman do his
work. She was rehearsing what she would say to
him, word and gesture both. There was anger in
her swinging walk, and in the carriage of the rosy
face and golden head which, in the shop lights,
called up the gay, or insolent, or sinister, or
merely stupid eyes of admiring men. Some knew
her, many called to her, "Hallo, pretty girl!"
She walked in the middle of the street, pouting,
out of humour, and made no answer. A young
fellow with a sheaf of seringa, more than half
faded, on his arm, the last unsold of his wares,
cried to her, "Flowers, buy my flowers! A sou
for the lot!" Weary, unsteady as a drunkard, the
young man lurched towards her; coming close,
and aware of the scent of shop-perfumery that
came from her, his Lyons street-wit impelled him
to call, "You don't want flowers—you're sweet
enough as you are!" She laughed cordially, she
felt herself to be looking well. Almost all her own
annoyance fell from her, with such little trace of
the grief of others as she had carried with her from
the convent. She went on by the bank of the
Rhone, under a million stars that scattered their
lights in the troubled waters. She went "home"
to her second-floor flat. When she entered the
kitchen a man in his shirt sleeves, leaning on the
window-sill, struck a match. He was a man of
thirty, with a rat face, glowing eyes, stiff moustache and hair. He held up the candle he had

lighted and looked at Ursula. His narrow face took a little colour, and his intelligent, untrustworthy eyes, eyes that changed expression much oftener than those of Ursula, sparkled with curiosity and enjoyment.

"Well?"

"I saw her."

"Did she turn you out?"

"That she didn't."

"I thought she would."

"I'm an old girl, remember."

"So you are; she let you in?"

"Yes, she did."

"When she heard they were going to shut up her old shop, she began to abuse the Government, I suppose?"

"No, she didn't."

"She cried, then?"

"Yes, poor old Sister. I didn't like it. I thought one time she was going to faint——"

"You mentioned the Mother-House?"

"Yes, as you told me."

"That's a good girl. And she just knocked under? It's a good joke, the way that fetches them—'Make the Mother-House safe.' You've done the job. So she promised to clear out without making a fuss, so as to save——"

"She didn't promise anything at all."

"Ah?"

"And you gave me your dirty work to do— that's what you did. I won't do any more. You can take it yourself."

He did not hear her. He was thinking.

"Come," he said laughing, "don't be cross.
We've done the trick. That's all that's wanted.
She didn't turn you out, and she won't make a
fuss. The governor will be pleased. Give us
a kiss."

II.

A VOCATION.

THE night had grown more moist, a night of the ripening of fruits, and its wings were over the cultivated lands. The blood of man and of the plant was renewed in the darkness. And the greater number of all creatures slept. In the house of the Sisters of St. Hildegarde the night lamp was not put out later than the customary hour. With those saintly souls, self-abandonment within the arms of Providence overcame grief. One after another the Sisters slept. One alone did not sleep, in an anguish that increased in the solitude of night—Pascale. Her childhood returned upon her, and the better she remembered her own brief yesterday, the more instant was her terror.

Her childhood returned upon her, and the close thereof—the painful close. Five years Pascale lived in a corner of the Croix Rousse, still called by old people in the district the "Pierres Plantées," nearly at the top of the Grande Côte, a street peopled by weavers, by second-hand dealers, butchers, grocers, bakers, whose little shops were narrow and deep; a street paved with cobbles after the ancient manner, too steep for any kind of carriage, and having notches cut

in the asphalt of its sidewalks so that foot-pas-
sengers should not have too many falls. She was
the child of one of the working quarters, the old
habitation of silk-weavers that is divided by the
Saône from the church quarter—Fourvière, with
its sanctuary standing over the mists of two great
rivers.

Pascale had carried away, in the depths of her
golden eyes, the image of her former world. She
beheld again, with a precision of remembrance
that moved her, as the thing itself had moved
her, that morning of December the 8th, 1897,
when she had resolved to utter, for the first time,
the secret that weighed upon her heart. A tardy
dawn was breaking. Neither on that night had
Pascale slept. She had watched for the first pal-
ing of the high window-pane—the one which,
seen from Pascale's bed below, had only the sky
beyond; and she had thought: "A fog again!
All day long to see the sun only through a heap
of mist! And I did pray for a fine day." And
then the electric looms had begun their beat,
beat, for the day, up above the Mouvands' flat,
on the second floor, for the three floors were inhabited by weavers, and for centuries floors, walls,
furniture, throughout the building, had shaken
all day long as though under the stress of a great
and incessant storm. Ah, silk enough had been
carried down that stair! Pieces enough of the
beautiful finished fabric had left those doors!
The shuttles had travelled many times round
the world.

The house, now newly fitted with machines,

was beginning a day's work, when a voice from
the distant workshop called:

"Pascale, do you hear them? Since they had
to pay seventy francs to the Jonage Works for
electric power, they make noise enough, those
Rambaux!"

"That's true."

"Did you sleep well?"

"Not so well as usual."

"I did, splendidly. I'm very fit to begin my
day. Make haste and dress—I'm ready."

And Pascale, rising in haste, felt that she was
shaken more profoundly than the building.

"I have to tell my father, who loves me so,
that I am to be a nun, that I am to leave him—
I must tell him, now, at once——."

She slipped on her woollen petticoat and stood
at the mirror-faced wardrobe, the only luxury of
her bedroom and only heritage from her mother,
and she unwound her hair. It was her chief
beauty, not because of its length, for it hardly
reached her waist, but for strength, vitality,
elastic abundance, and the flame of colour that
played here and there through its fairness; it
looked a very crown of youth, and its brightness
lighted the pale face of the city work-girl. The
slightest movement of her head made the lights
flow over those spreading tresses, which resembled handfuls of Chinese or Japanese silk prepared
for the embroidering of golden birds flying, or
golden fish swimming, on the ground of some blue
screen. Often and often had she looked with delight on her own hair, this tender Pascale; it

smiled at her. She had nursed, as she looked, those thoughts of vanity that are, in their source, neither more nor less than the desires of love. But for some months past she had denied herself such dreams, and on this morning she had no difficulty in keeping them away. By the light of her little night-lamp she saw her mirrored eyes, dull and sleepless. "And what will they look like when I have said all I have to say—when I have cried, as I shall cry?" she wondered. But it mattered little. She made haste to fasten up her hair and to dress herself.

Whence had this girl a convent vocation? In the first place, from a rare self-knowledge. Her mother, dead three years before, a working woman with eyes full of prayer and of dreams, a face wide at the brow and narrow at the chin, and a figure bent, from her earliest years, over the loom, that patient "hand" who was reluctant to undertake intricate patterns because of the mental effort they demanded—her mother had bequeathed her an anxious temperament, a heart sensitive to excess, a passionate love of children and much timidity in regard to men. Pascale, less sheltered than her mother by daily indoor labour, a pupil of the Sisters until the age of thirteen, and afterwards busy about the house, the kitchen, the marketing, while her parents were at their weaving, had noted how quickly her own nature was moved by affectionate words, by the happy or painful confidences of her friends, by the sentimental lessons of the few romances she had read, by attentions, looks, signs of harmless admiration, of evil desires, by the tumult of feeling, like the concourse in the street at eleven o'clock, agitations of human emotion that touched her nearly, embarrassed her, and flattered her.

She felt the shock and the trouble when she went out to fetch the milk or the vegetables, when she met, on the stairs, the insolent young men of the Rambaux family, dwellers on the third floor, who, in her honour only, stood aside and raised their caps; and when the agents of M. Talier-Décapy came to inspect the works, to place orders, or to summon Mouvand to the owner's room. She felt the attraction, she felt the fear. She dreaded to appear, to be praised, to mix with the crowd, to feel herself coveted, to breathe that breath of passion from the street which all town-dwellers must meet, but which beats so hotly on the faces of the young and of the lovely. Her thrills, her curiosity, her uneasiness revealed its own frailty to her watchful heart. She was alarmed, for this was a religious girl, who prized her own chastity as a treasure. One day she pronounced in her own secret counsels her own sentence: "I believe I should be more easily ruined than other girls. I ought to take refuge." And this thought came and came again.

Pascale observed herself also on the point of obedience. She knew herself uncertain, doubtful, reluctant, slow to act, harassed by regrets when she had acted even in trivial things; but full of peace under the yoke of a reasonable obedience. Her father's word, her mother's, or that of another in whom she trusted—"This is the right thing, this you should do"—cleared the doubt and quieted the questioning. Then and not till then did she set about the work before her. It might always be her lot to follow directions that she could trust and love. She was one of a great multitude of human souls that have neither greatness nor strength except through their affections. Doubtless she might have married, and often by her as by other girls that future had been faced. It was the common lot—a husband, a house, children. But she had not been educated in the illusion that marriage and happiness are one. She had seen the fate of women otherwise. Daughter of a mother early dead, sister of a little Blandine destroyed by meningitis at ten years old, herself delicate and subject to long-lasting winter coughs, she could not think of marriage without remembering the exhaustion of young women under frequent child-birth, and under the concurrent necessity of bread-winning for themselves and others; without remembering the still less fortunate among her neighbours—forsaken, beaten, bound for life to idlers and to ruffians.

And even had she been sought in marriage by a good man, an industrious weaver and son of weavers—as there were not a few in the Croix Rousse—or by a clerk or little tradesman, would the protection of her youth be effectual? "If I don't grow bad," she thought, "I shall not be very good. In that commonplace life, subject to influences as I am, I may still have vague wishes for something more perfect, but I shall not rise. I should be much safer in a convent. I should

have the safeguard of the nunnery walls, the safeguard of examples, of the rule, of regular obligatory
prayer. In the world I might be a bad woman
or a very ordinary one; in the convent I might
become a saintly soul. Is not that the one thing
for me?"

She had asked this question of a friend whose
counsel she valued. This was a woman whose
work in the silk-weaving industry was the spinning
of one thread with another—the "joining on" for
the continuing of a single piece of silk. For this
task she came once or twice a month, and it required exceeding cleanliness, skill, attention, and
practice. So many silken fibres to unite, so that
they should be, beyond all detection, continuous!
This widow Flachat, a discreet person of very
respectable poverty, used to come in the morning,
bringing the milk which she had bought in a trust-
worthy dairy, and set straight about her work.
Her face was bent over it and raised no more.
Into the milk she dipped her thumb and her index
finger, and with them twisted the two threads
that seemed to melt under her touch into one.
She took her food in the house, as the custom
is, and it was easy for Pascale, when her father
left the room, to consult the "tordeuse," who
had the art of listening as well as the art of her
own work.

"I am not surprised at what you tell me, my
little Pascale," she said, "and your mother would
have been glad to hear it. She liked church
services."

"Well, but I don't," cried Pascale, laughing;

"I get tired in church. I am not quite what you think me, Madame Flachat."

"I know what I mean," continued the woman, twisting her threads. "I mean that your mother was like you, anxious to be better than the rest of us, and bound to have trouble. I have been through the world, my girl, and I can tell you that it is not an easy place. Are you thinking of a convent?"

"Yes, thinking—but I don't exactly wish for it."

"Like a marriage one is just wondering about."

"Something like that."

"Well, my dear, go on—don't be in a hurry, don't be anxious. If your heart is inclined that way, let it go."

She spoke like wisdom itself, and Pascale thought and thought again.

And then it was that in the pure, the doubtful, the diffident soul of Pascale Mouvand arose the wish for a cloistered life, wherein she believed peace and security awaited her, that environment of tenderness, without deceit, without betrayal, of which the dream had been born with her. No sudden illumination, no mystic ardour, no vapour of incense, no dazzle of azure and gold, no miraculous love of self-sacrifice led Pascale to the cloister, but only the deliberate conviction that no other way of life could so well develop what was good in her and so well safeguard what was perilous. She was afraid, she had seen the shelter, she sought it. The thought of leaving her father gave her pain, but this other thought overcame it: that the

conditions of safety are not alike for all human
souls, but that they are imperious, that they are
not to be judged by the faithless, and that there
is no duty on earth that may stand against them.

A religious vocation was no startling thing to
befall this family. That old race of Lyons silk-
weavers was even as its last descendants, laborious, scanty of speech, ardent at heart, capable of
long patience but also of terrible revolt, devout
and home-keeping. Despite so much effort to
glorify ignorance or hatred of religion in the poor,
it kept its place in the foremost rank of those
numerous families in the Croix Rousse, in the
Guillotière, or in Saint-Irénée, who look to the
sanctuary of Fourvière for help, and to the Virgin
as a friend to them and to their town. The
Mouvands had taken part in the foundation of the
ancient charity of the Hospital Watchers, created
by the workmen of Lyons in 1767; and at the
beginning of the twentieth century, Adolphe
Mouvand held that he did himself honour by a
Sunday visit to the hospitals, where he shaved and
combed and brushed the poor patients as his
maternal great-great-uncle, Jean Marie Moncize-
rand, had done of old. He had brought up his
children—he must now, alas! say his child—in
the tradition of practical religion, to which he had
remained faithful. He would not refuse his consent to Pascale's wish; he would not long oppose
her. But as yet she had not told him. She had
left him, through pity, out of the struggle, out of
the doubt, out of the dismay that so troubled her.
For their characters were all unlike. He sus-

pected nothing. And his surprise, his grief, perhaps his anger, when he should know her secret—it was the apprehension of these that for many nights, and for this night just past, had kept Pascale awake.

When she had fastened her dress and pinned up her hair, she threw over her shoulders a cape of silky wool, entirely black, that had been her mother's, brought the edges together at her throat with a little metal bar set with false turquoises; and, as she belonged to a generation that was "prideful," as the weaver said, she drew on her brown kid gloves.

Then she had so violent a beating of the heart that she needed to lean against her bedstead, one hand upon her breast. "Oh, tell me what I ought to say," she whispered. Slowly she opened her door. The adjoining room, her father's, was vacant. Pascale crossed it, turned at right angles, and entered the large workshop of the weaver. The Rambaux were at work above; otherwise her step on the old floor would have been audible. Adolphe Mouvand was not at his usual place, on the bench before the first loom, but at the end of the workshop near the other machine which stood dusty and motionless always, the old loom at which his wife had worked. No one for three years had been allowed to touch this relic. The weaver placed his hand—a small hand, expert at holding the shuttle in the palm—upon the wood, polished with much usage. He looked at it all—the frame, the uprights, the cardboard still hanging, on which was traced the last pattern woven

by the dead. Mouvand had his face towards the
windows. The light, incomparably higher in tone
here than on the river levels of the city, struck out
the outline of the master-weaver's arched head
and square face, with its thick and strong grey
beard pushed forward by his habitual attitude at
work, with his chin turned in towards his breast.
He wore his black holiday clothes. Amongst his
hard, short hair some locks whiter than the rest
shone like silvery antique plush. He was deep in
thought and did not hear his child. But his down-
ward-sweeping eyes caught the sudden shadow on
the boards. And he saw Pascale, and all his soul
put work and the loom aside, and his eyebrows
gathered into a frown as though she had surprised
him in some fault. But this was but a momentary
effect of instinct. To his grave and weighty face
came joy; it lightened in his eyes, those laborious
eyes so long dimmed like the sky of the town;
made them larger; slightly rosied the parchment
of his cheek; and showed, beneath his moustache,
the bold, ironic lips that had launched so many
cheerful words on the Lyons air, on holidays, or
in times of strike or of a lock-out, when he met
his friends in the wine-shop or played a game at
bowls on the heights of the Croix Rousse. In the
twinkling of an eye the face, the thought, and
the attitude of Adolphe Mouvand had changed.
And it was seldom indeed that he thus shone out
of the sequestered place of his reserve. It was
the image of Pascale that transformed him, the
beloved Pascale, coming to him dressed for the
street.

"Well, Pretty," said he, for he often called her so. "You startled me."

He leant forward to look at her with his worn eyes.

"But what a face! How pale you look! It's not Ash Wednesday, little girl. It's our own Virgin's holiday, and you and I shall eat fritters together."

He kissed her on both cheeks with a smack.

"Shall you like it—a little treat of fritters? We'll buy them after Mass, at Bellefin's, where they are good. I shall enjoy going out with you. Say, shall you like it?"

She was embarrassed by his great good humour. She kissed her father, and her words died in the kiss—her cruel words.

"Do you know what I was thinking of? I was thinking of you," he said. "Yes, as I handled your mother's loom, I said to myself that you would never manage it. It's all right for me, and it was all right for her. My old body and my old machine are good companions. But you—you are not strong enough."

"I don't think I am."

"And then you have no fancy for it."

She smiled and said:

"Nor the time either."

But he grasped nothing yet, and followed his own thought.

"You are right; your mother would not have me teach you to weave the fine silks; so I said to her, 'Then she shall not do common work either,' and so we taught you none of it. And

you were delicate—and we spoilt you between us.
You learnt nothing at home but keeping house,
but that you did well, little girl."

He paused for a minute, as it were lapping her
in the tenderness of his thoughts:

"But listen now. Old men change their minds
sometimes. I mean to give in after all, and have
electric power in my workshop. We'll sell the
mother's loom, and you shall just be a kind of
overseer. Or you can try your hand at a little
easy work—ribbons, if you like. We shall be
better off. What do you think?"

She answered, turning to the street, whence the
light was increasing:

"You are too kind to me. But come, or we
shall miss Mass."

They descended the staircase, which had windows fitted with nothing but iron bars. It was
as windy there as in the street.

"Take care and cover your chest; these stairs
have killed some of us. And you, Pretty, you've
got to live."

She went down before him, holding her cape
close to her shoulders and her bust. She went
lightly in the fresh and animating air, and jumped
the three last stone steps, as though to show that
she was much alive and that her youth was not
failing her. Together the father and daughter
heard Mass at St. Bernard's, which is on the
heights of the Croix Rousse, and then, as the
father had said, they went down to the Rue
Tables Claudiennes, where was the shop and frying
kitchen, for the promised fritters. Mouvand ate

his share in the street; Pascale asked for a paper bag.

"That's our young ladies of the day, all over, Bellefin," he cried, "they won't live in public."

The man within put his head out of his narrow shop, with an expert old eye scanning Pascale.

"I haven't got one like her," he said. "You are a lucky fellow to be cutting a dash in town with a daughter of that kind. What's her age?"

"More than eighteen," replied Pascale.

"And a voice! Say it again, it's like singing— and I'll put an extra fritter into this bag of yours."

"Eighteen, Monsieur Bellefin, eighteen, eighteen!"

For the first time she laughed out. This Bellefin was droll, and had a nice way of talking to girls. She laughed, with her fresh lips apart, smooth as the lining of a shell; and she repeated, with her eyes on the old bonze in his hollow niche, feeling that she was made free of the street and of the morning, "Eighteen years old and more! Now, Monsieur Bellefin, give me my fritter with extra sugar on it."

It was as though the two men stood listening to a blackbird that one of them had been training, or to a piping bullfinch performing at a competition: "Aha, that's a note for you! It would have been a pity not to take pains with this little creature."

On their way back up the hill Adolphe Mouvand felt that he had never before loved Pascale so much, nor loved her so proudly. At the corner of the Rue Tables Claudiennes, he said:

"There, go back home to your business; I

have a good deal to do, so don't expect me to dinner. But be sure to be up at the Fourvière church at one o'clock, when the bell rings for the men to go in."

They separated and spent the rest of the morning apart. Mouvand had always balanced his accounts on the eighth of December, and this implied several payments, two or three visits to old weavers retired or invalided, and a déjeuner at half past eleven with Constant Mury, a strong socialist of the Croix Rousse, a stout old weaver who presided over the bowling ground of the Pierres Plantées. Before one o'clock he was at the Place de la Cathédrale at the foot of the hill of Fourvière. The open space was black with a solid crowd of men, stationary there, but still moving at the openings of the Rue St. Jean, of the Rue Antonine, and of the Rue de la Brèche, whence new comers poured in. There were none but men in the gathering, five or six thousand. Soon there would be a thousand more, and together they would march up the zig-zag road to the Holy Hill, to manifest in the sanctuary of their city their civic faith.

The weaver greeted his mates here and there. "I told Pascale the procession would be a good one. What a crowd! The little girl must be up at the church by now." He did not go with the rest, having rheumatic pains in his back that made the long march too hard for him, but went up by the funicular railway to the high platform, the place of refuge, the place near to Heaven, where the basilica raises over the city her four tall towers, the crown of Lyons. He did not know it then, but this hill was his Calvary. How often do we go even so, carrying our joys with hardly a tremor, in spite of chance, to the obscure place where their unsuspected close awaits us! This man's heart was more free than was usual with him. He had unaccustomed leisure, and had that morning been long away from the home within which at times he had wept. His cheerful humour had been increased by companionship at Constant Mury's. As he paid his swo sous to the man at the funicular, he said:

"Your lift doesn't cost much, but it's a little way. Have you seen my girl?"

"I've seen a lot of girls, but I am not sure about yours."

"A pretty one—mine is," said Mouvand. "Fair hair, and a fresh cheek—not many quite like her. And a wing in her hat!"

He was right about the hat. To please him on the holiday, Pascale had put on her felt hat with a grey wing in it. She was waiting for her father in front of the church. She walked quickly at his side to the place where the head of the procession would soon appear. From below, the bell—the *bourdon*—of Saint Jean had rung the note that signalled "They are moving." And now the great bell of the Fourvière mountain, that of the south-east tower, pealed aloud to hail the foremost pilgrims of the march.

They came up bare-headed, filling the whole breadth of the street, almost every man reciting the rosary. The road cast them out opposite

the nave of the church, and there they turned
to the right, passing slowly with a loud noise of
prayers and footsteps through the cloister of the
old chapel, and thence into the modern basilica,
according to the order prescribed. It was all male
Lyons that had climbed the hill—factory hands,
shopmen, clerks, the rich, the poor, gathered
without class or distinction. And the great
bell spread its deep voice over the sounds of
the city—a triumphal wave, rolling above the
smoke, clearing the mist, reaching far ahead,
far back, many a mile, over the tableland
of the Dombes, across the plain of the Rhone,
along the hills beyond Ecully and Saint Foy.
Then suddenly the carillon of the tower on
the right, with its eleven brass notes, rang
out the tunes of the Virgin's hymns. The men
sang within the basilica, and outside. And
while this pilgrim army was on the march, all
the rocks of that great hill, all the stones of its
houses, all the bones of the living and of the
buried dead upon the heights vibrated to the
sound of the prayer that was spoken, was sung,
was tolled.

At the end of the church Pascale, who had
slipped in with the crowd at her father's side,
stood against the base of one of the white marble
piers of the nave. All the chairs had been re-
moved, and the sombre-coloured crowd of men,
filling the whole space, gave still greater brilliance
to the coloured decoration of walls and roof, the
mosaics, the glass, the gilding, the great light
shadow all alive with reflections that played and

mingled together like the colours of an opal. A
hymn was sung. The cardinal entered and passed
before the ranks. A priest made a short speech.
The throng was moved with a common feeling
that was not all devotion; it was also the sense of
power and of fraternity, of corporate union in
religious things, habitual to the forefathers of
these men—their condition of daily life—but to
these a matter of momentary experience. Fre-
quenters of a score of churches, accustomed to
meet by mere groups, used to the life of single
or solitary will, it was suddenly only, and briefly,
that they became consciously an army. And
in that gathering each unit prayed his best; the
stranger was to him a brother; neighbours forgot
their differences; it was the acknowledgement
of a common hope, in a common humiliation,
before a common Father. And the prospect of a
common future suggested between these strangers
something of courtesy, something of respect, and
something of the tryst eternity.

Adolphe Mouvand was deep in the solid life of
the people of his city, was by heredity and environment one of them, and he could not fail to
feel the expansion of happiness and pride; he
sang aloud, he listened, he held up his head; and
his eyes, used to the daily sight of machines and
bare walls, beheld, wherever they glanced within
that church, the light of Paradise. He forgot to
look at Pascale. Like the rest, he knew nothing
of the symbolism of angels with open wings, of
peacocks with outspread tails, but he was well
aware that his city had added a new stanza to an

old hymn, by raising to the Virgin a modern church far superior, both in feeling and in art, to such new churches as have no soul unborrowed from the past.

The young girl on her part saw nothing, absorbed as she was by the thought that distressed her. She had leaned her head against the marble pier, and had closed her eyes; she was in trouble, for the hour was near, and she was motionless, as though for fear that a movement might bring the hand of the clock to the dreadful moment. Calls for help uttered themselves within her: "Oh, my God! it breaks my heart to hurt him. Nothing could take me from him but Thy own call. I know I need Thy shelter and the cover of holy friendships, for I have no will of my own but the will to submit to those I care for. Help me, because even now my cowardly spirit would escape! Strengthen me, because he has so many rights over me that I am ashamed to speak of my rights over myself. And yet, if I married, should I not have to leave him? Help me to speak, help him to hear me!"

The crowd was now passing away. All those near her had risen, had left the church and descended the steps beyond the great bronze doors, when Pascale slowly raised her hand and laid it on her father's shoulder.

"Whenever you like, Pretty," said the weaver, rousing himself. "I am ready."

He was turning to leave the place, but feeling her detaining hand, he asked, "What do you want to say to me?"

And he leant his ear close to the mouth that looked so pale.

"Father, I want to speak to you here because God is close to us——"

She was trying to break the news to him, but her secret was too much for her strength; it overcame, it spoke:

"Forgive me. I want to be a nun."

"A nun? What are you talking about?"

He saw that she had turned ashen pale, and the words he had been about to speak were dumb within him.

"Is it true? Do you mean it?"

She made a frightened sign of affirmation, as though she dreaded that a more positive reply might kill him. But to her great surprise Pascale did not see him stagger, nor did she feel him grow rigid in anger. He did but draw himself somewhat towards the altar, and replied not to her but to One who had spoken by her mouth.

"My God! is it possible? I never thought—a nun—my girl!"

And as though her wish had already sounded the very depths of his being—the place where will abides—Mouvand said, with his eyes still on the golden door on the altar:

"Is it for hospital work that you are to leave me, Pascale?"

"No, father, I shall go to the Sisters of St. Hildegarde."

"To teach children?"

The low voice answered:

"To save my soul."

The two were silent for so long a time as the saying of an Ave Maria might cover. Then Pascale, raising her eyes, beheld that wonderful thing, by her undreamed of—the victory of a great faith even at the moment of the falling of the blow. All his saintly race, all his faithful fathers, dead and saved, doubtless prayed for the weaver. From his own eyes fell two tears, and yet his face was not saddened. Nay, rather joy grew there, and the soul looked out, content, submissive. But a long moment passed before he could speak again. Then he said, with his face still turned to the altar:

"I will not grudge you to God, Pascale. You shall go where you wish."

Then he took his daughter in one stout arm— he was a man of lively blood, unaccustomed to much meditating—and drew her out of the church through the open doors of bronze, and down the steps, the last of all the pilgrims, sheltering and holding to his heart this child promised to God. It was a King going forth with a young Queen.

When they were in the *place* she said:

"How kind you are! I was afraid to tell you."

He replied in his great voice:

"Silly! Afraid of me?"

"I couldn't sleep; I made up my mind to tell you in the morning."

"Before Mass?"

"Yes."

"You did look—funny. And how long have you meant to be a nun?"

"Two years and more."

"Is that why you got me to go to Vespers so often?"

"Yes, that was it."

"And why you wouldn't go to the wedding of the girl on the first floor?"

"Well, perhaps."

"And why you wouldn't let me buy you a brooch for your birthday?"

"Yes."

"And I never guessed. How easy it is to hoodwink a father! I used to say, 'Well, perhaps there's someone in love with her.' You might have had someone—a good many—in love with you?"

She laughed. She knew that it was so. They turned into the Rue Juge de Paix, which skirts the town towards the west.

"If you had thought of marrying, Pretty, you'd have had admirers enough. I think young Rambaux would have had you?"

"*I* wouldn't have had *him*."

"Well, he is not worth very much. He works, but that's not everything. It doesn't make a man altogether. I know others who had a fancy for Pascale."

"You had, first of all," she said, thanking him with a look.

Meanwhile the thought of parting, kept off for a while, slipped into the weaver's mind with many another. Sorrow entered into joy. But the bitter graft did not at once take hold; and the tree of happiness flourished.

"All the same, I was very happy in living together, Pascale. It was not quite the same thing to you, may be?"

"Oh, yes, it was!"

"Since we lost your mother, it is quite likely I've been out rather too often on Sundays."

"Oh no."

"Played bowls too much? Perhaps I should have taken out my Pascale?"

"Well, I should have enjoyed it, but that would not have changed my mind."

"What made you think of it first?"

She said, shaking her head:

"I felt myself to be very weak."

He understood nothing, being very little used to look at things from within, and he merely made a sign of assent. They were walking between walls rusty or green with moss, the walls of convents or of mission houses and alms-houses, and the road turned and turned, but silence was complete around them. Here and there an overhanging bough of plane or elder tree blessed the wayfarer.

Pascale, once more absorbed in her perpetual thought, but now at ease and even joyous, walked some hundred paces without speaking; and then, feeling that her father had not quite understood her, she added:

"You see, I want a rule, if I am really to be good."

"You were good enough for me," said the weaver, in a low voice. But he quickly added, to correct the blasphemy: "I know there is An-

other not so easily pleased. Pascale, I say it
again, I shall not stand against it. No, I promise
you that."

Both workman and child together were light
of heart, and their joy was devout, but it was
also hasty. They knew it to be eternal in its
source, but transitory in their human hearts.
And both hoped to reach the country of the future
where it would be lasting; and they had no
shadow of doubt that they were acting according
to the order and the will that are divine.

"A nun—" repeated Mouvand. "No, when
the time comes, I shall not stop her."

When the time comes—here was grief revisiting
the father's heart. Pascale had not told him
when she must go. Her father had not asked her.
The stress of feeling had hidden the distress. He
tried to evade the question arising within him,
the question growing instant, soon to become
agonising—"When will she go? When will she
leave me alone?" He said:

"I don't rightly recollect any nun in our family,
except only a great-grandaunt. But that was
so far back—I heard of it when I was a child."

The Rue Juge de Paix and the Rue Quatre
Vents were reddened by the sunset. Near to its
final decline, the sun passed quickly through
the lurid mists, piercing them with outlets of
crimson and gold over which the clouds again
gathered, to be again shot through. Pascale and
her father were now before the gateway of the
great cemetery of Loyasse, on the western summit and slope of the height. They were making

their customary visit to a grave, for on each
eighth of December Adolphe Mouvand came
hither; and to-day he was urged by something
more than habit. The district of Saint Irénée,
close by, had been the cradle of his race. The
graves of the old weavers were there, or had been,
for the poor have none but temporary homes in
the burial-ground, and are turned away from
their graves when the rent is over-due, as they
were from their houses when they lived, from
their poor rooms, or from the workshops of their
masters.

Between two little pollard trees stood side by
side the crosses of the grandfather and the mother
of Pascale. By the principal avenue of leafless
sycamores the father and daughter reached the
limit of the plateau containing the *Concessions
perpétuelles*, the graves of private ownership that
would never be disturbed; thence began the steep
incline, black above, fringed with white below.
For here lay the poor, adults in the upper part,
children at the foot, and the graves were covered
with black bead wreaths on the hill and white in
the valley. The man and the girl had brought
new wreaths for their dead, and they knelt, having
spread their handkerchiefs under their knees, and
their prayer was fervent and full of life and truth.
The face of the weaver grew tender, his beard
moved as though he spoke, he passed his hand
across his eyes to control his tears. Then he rose,
and with his knife began to trim the grave, over-
grown and neglected for lack of time to spare, and
because of the great distance. To Pascale kneel-

ing alone it seemed that something of herself, of
her heart or her thought, something tender, was
finding a way through the wet grass and reaching
the ear of the dead woman, saying: "Mother, I
am going to the convent; I have come to tell
you. Give me your blessing. I am like you, I
feel so much. Don't be uneasy for me. I shall
have less to suffer where I am go'ng than you had
in your married life, Mother. I think perhaps it
was you who deserved that I should have this
better life. I shall pray for you, and that will be
my way of coming to you, for I shall hardly be
able to come up to Loyasse. You will know that
I am all right. I wish, Mother, you could have
seen me in my veil. You would have cried, though.
You would have understood, all the same. I give
you a kiss through the earth and the stones. I
am your child, and I thank you for all my childhood that has brought me to this."

She rose. Her father, who had begun to think
of home by the cross of his wife, closed the blade
of his knife, which snapped with a click, and said:

"You are very young, Pascale; there's no hurry.
When do you think of beginning?"

They were now walking back along the avenue.
At first she answered nothing, in pity for him,
and next she took his arm so that her caress
might assure him of her love.

"You are very young," he said again.

A little further yet they walked, and leaving
Loyasse they followed the road that leads to the
right by the old fortifications. Mouvand was
waiting, in much trouble, for her reply. She felt

that he was pressing her arm as though to say: "Come, Pretty, out with it. I know, I understand."

She said: "I should like to go in at Christmas —into the novitiate."

"At Christmas, Pascale! At Christmas I shall be without you!"

Steadfast as he was, and gay, and not used to complain or accuse, he was forced to stop; he breathed hard, his eyes closed as though he had made an effort too great for his strength.

"Oh!" cried Pascale, "don't make me cry; I am such a weak creature, even when I see my duty clearly enough; and if you let me see how sorry you are, I might not go at all. And all the while I am quite sure that God calls me."

Adolphe Mouvand was one to whom reverence for the name of God gave strength against himself.

"You are right," he said at once, but slowly. "I must be brave. It is a great blessing to us."

"How well you understand, father!"

"Yes—a great favour. I try to do right with my hospital work; but this is better. Well, Pascale, you must not sacrifice your youth to my age. Go and live your right life, as our fathers lived theirs—they knew the way, Pascale!"

He had been so thoroughly trained in ideal and habitual religion that the highest and most ideal thoughts on duty, on conduct, on the aims of the soul, were to him familiar. As he spoke the weaver went up the crest of the table-land, the place once a fortress of the Romans, and still bearing, on the west, traces of the long glacis and walls. Pascale had followed her father, and was resting her hand on the stones of the parapet.

He stretched forth his arm. "There," he said, "is Saint Irénée, where all the Mouvands came from, and there is the town. But we can't quite see our own place from here."

Before and below them in a deep fold of the valley, the old working district of Saint Irénée, coloured a soft, faded pink, thronged its houses together, so closely that here and there two or three looked as though they had been lifted— ever so little—above the rest by the pressure. Over them all floated the misty smoke. A steep, wooded height rose beyond, and further than the tree tops again were hills and more hills, vaguer and vaguer in the fading light, following the rivers into which their spurs were dipped. On that side, very low down to the left, lay what Mouvand called the "town." But it was the town and something more. Beyond the invisible Saône, where it turned by the rocks of Fourvière and Saint Just, lay the whole southern part of the huge city, the peninsula of Perrache, the Rhone, the point of the district of La Guillotière, the district of La Mouche; meadows mingled with building and with scattered poplars; green country with no limit except the dusky mist; and the great river, made of the Saône and the Rhone together, catching the light and then passing into the dimness, on its journey to the south.

Pascale and her father looked down at the town. It was veiled by a transparent fog, coloured by the evening. Five hundred thousand human creatures were there. It was their breath, full of their many sufferings, it was the smoke of their hearths and of their machinery, it was the dust of their use and their activity, that formed this cloud. The tangled noises of the multitude rose with it. Father and daughter, beholding this apparition of their own city, were silent. The weaver thought of his toil, of which the odour and the vibration were about his fancy again, drawing him down to his little private cell in the hive before him. It was his; it was empty. He shook his head and muttered in his beard:

"Not to-day. This is a holiday. And to-morrow will be a holiday too, because of the little girl—a holiday for old Mouvand."

But that city fog enclosed cries and lamentations, the breath of the sick and the fever-stricken, words of hatred, words of revolt, cries of despair. And Pascale, who was going into the Convent "to save her soul," but to save it by devoting it, understood that mingling of human voices, opened her breast to that tide of pain, filled her being, filled her heart, as she thought: "Miseries are there below such as I shall help. I shall teach the children at any rate, and they will surely love me. I shall be their mother always." And her heart dilated and was so happy that she would have stayed there long had not her father stirred his great iron-bound boots.

"Come, Pretty, we have a long way to go."

They said no more, but the course of their thoughts had changed. Pascale's vocation, now certain, absorbed all her power of dreaming; the

old weaver, an enthusiast, and a child despite his
years, little spoilt by life, was looking forward to
making a good use of the days before Pascale's
departure. He filled them in anticipation with
treats for Pascale, with excursions. For the first
time he thought with excitement of the coming
holidays. He was dazzled.

Pascale and her father followed the road of
the fortifications as far as the gate of St. Irénée.
Night had now fully come; the fog that had been
parted by the dying sun met again and closed his
tomb. It was heavy on men's shoulders. Mouvand, who was not fond of the open air at this
hour, when, as he said, "bad things fall on us,"
proposed a supper at an inn he knew in the lower
part of Saint Irénée. They entered under the
great gateway, and sought the inn, its shelter and
warmth.

When they again left it, seven o'clock was
near. Restored after the fatigue of the day,
glad to have had more than usual intimacy in
their talk, pleased with the luxury of holiday
food, they went quickly down the steep streets
from Saint Irénée to the quays of the Saône.
They were midway on the foot-bridge that creaks
under the feet of wayfarers, when at the stroke
of seven all the bells of the city took flight. They
cried, "Light up!" And in a moment the lines
of gas lights multiplied. Above, below, aloft, in
the invisible façades of innumerable houses to
the right, to the left, new lines and curves of lights
sprang upon the night. They appeared with
strange quickness and caprice, breaking up the

customary form of bridges, squares, and streets.
Windows, archways, doorways were traced in fire.
The quays sparkled, the heights of Fourvière were
enkindled; the belfry of the old church rose in
golden stars from the heart of the darkness; a
luminous cross, erect on the terrace of the basilica,
raised its arms over the city; the Archbishop's
house became a palace of fire; inscriptions came
out in lights on the hill-side: *"Lyon à Marie"*—
"Maria Mater Dei"—*"Dieu protège la France."*
Garlands, festoons, lamps in drinking glasses,
Venetian lanterns, candles stuck into the necks of
bottles, flickered in the wind of little by-streets, of
cross-roads and squares, telling those who might
have doubted that the slums were full of souls,
and the huge city of faith. Not Fourvière only,
but the whole of Lyons was illuminated.

Pascale, delighted, Mouvand, very demonstrative, took one street and then another, followed
random groups, left them, returned often to the
Saône, and went on still unsatisfied with seeing.

"How beautiful the illumination is this year!"
they said to one another. "Let's go now and
see whether the Bourbonnes have lighted up, and
the Boffards. When we go home, we'll see
whether the Seignemontes have any lamps out."
And lamps were everywhere. The distant hill
of the Croix Rousse seemed to be sprinkled with
sparks. La Guillotière looked as phosphorescent
as the sea. "All the stars are on earth to-night,"
said the weaver; "it is a pretty holiday." In fact,
there were neither moon nor stars in the skies, but
only the cloud of fog and mist lighted from be-

neath and tinted now by man, as before by the sun.

Long wandered Adolphe Mouvand with Pascale upon his arm in the innumerable multitude that the illumination and the shops had called into the streets. They exchanged words and thoughts, having no secrets, and with an infinite sweetness. Of some poor scanty past pleasures they spoke, with recollections and allusions that had no meaning but for themselves. But now and then, at the close of this great day of the revelation of the soul, a religious thought, an idea of sacrifice and of Paradise, came to one or the other. They were like two neighbour chapels whence rose the notes of the self-same hymn. They loved each other more than ever, and were not shy in telling each other that dear truth. And when they went home, late at night, father and daughter could have wept for joy because of the grief which together they had accepted and taken home.

On the following morning Adolphe Mouvand drew near to Pascale, who was lighting the stove for the warming of the coffee, and said, rubbing his hands:

"I have an idea—it's my turn." He struck his pocket. "I had put some coins away—not many. I should be sorry to spend them without you. What do you say to taking a journey?"

"Well—where?"

"As far as Nîmes, where our only living relatives are—the Prayous. You never saw them, but you shall see them now. Three days' holiday, Mouvand, my boy, like a gentleman!"

"Just what I should love," said the happy Pascale. "A journey! It will give me something to talk about, later on, to my little girls."

He had but to write to the Prayous, and to finish a piece of silk he had promised; and in the morning, two days later, the weaver and his daughter took the train for the South.

They set forth in fog; they reached Nîmes in the splendour of a winter day, in the clear, thrilling, living cold of the mistral wind.

"How keen it is!" said Mouvand, putting his hand out of the carriage window.

"How bright it is!" said Pascale; "like the summer light with us."

The castle of Tarascon, the castle of Beaucaire, the Rhone between them, with the reflections of each castled hill in the sunny river; then the walls of old enclosures, built foursquare, looking like fortresses, with their straight cypresses—lances planted in the soil and keeping guard to the north; next, the first houses of Nîmes, white in the sun— all were mirrored in Pascale's golden eyes. As to the weaver, he seldom glanced through the carriage windows; he smoked, looking continually at his child—two true pleasures. Father and daughter had spoken little on the journey, but each had felt that joy of another which brings peace to the gentle heart.

At the Nîmes station, hardly were they on the platform when a stout woman, black-haired and swarthy, ran up to the weaver and noisily kissed him.

"There you are! Why, it *was* a surprise! I

never thought I should see you again, cousin.
And little Pascale, where is she? What, this great
girl? And to think I saw her when she was three!
Well, she *is* a brave lass!"

"And a pretty one, too," said a voice behind
her.

Pascale smiled before she saw the speaker, and
smiled again when she perceived a tall young man
of slender figure, very pale, very young, with the
regular beauty of a statue in the upper part of
his face, but a prominent, coarse jaw. A short
moustache and curly beard partly concealed this
ominous lower part of a handsome face, and the
sinuous lips. The eyes were soft as velvet. The
man held out his hand.

"Mademoiselle," he said, showing his teeth,
"will you excuse me? Here at Nîmes, when we
admire a beautiful girl we have to let her know
it."

"There is no offence in that," said Pascale.
Flattered, she gave him her hand, while his mother
kissed the young girl, and seized her valise.

"Ah! the rogue, he's a judge. And only
twenty! Would you think it? This way—we
live quite near. And what do you think of the
South?"

"Well, I think it is cold," said the weaver.

"Just a touch of the mistral, a touch of the
broom that sweeps our Rhone valley," said the
young man, who had taken his place at Pascale's
side and walked on with her, while behind came
the weaver in his horn-buttoned jacket and the
stout woman, bareheaded, with a scanty knot of

hair and wide partings between her oily locks.
She had the muscles, the appearance, and the
bearing of a professional swimmer. She carried
the valise, of which every now and then Mouvand
offered to relieve her. Jules Prayou walked
empty-handed and showed Pascale the town;
the fine plane-trees—now leafless—of the Feu-
chère avenue, the esplanade and the Pradier
fountain, and the amphitheatre, which they
skirted. The wind was high; it swathed the
women's petticoats about their legs.

"It does push one," said Pascale. "It seems
to want to hurry me into your Rue de Montpellier."

"You shall see finer streets to-morrow," said
Jules Prayou; "this is only an old one. See!
here is the hospital."

He pointed out a monumental doorway fram-
ing bars through which were visible a further and
smaller barred gateway, and ancient buildings sur-
rounding a square.

"My late husband died here," said the widow
in a religious tone, from behind.

"Did he leave you comfortable, cousin?" asked
the weaver, whose sensibilities were not very
ready at call.

"Well, something; a little plot, some olive
trees. But that big fellow there is an expense,
Monsieur Mouvand."

"What does he do? No work?"

The woman answered in her Southern way with
a vivacious gesture, as though to signify that he
had a great variety of employments, all of uncertain profit; she gathered together the five

fingers of her left hand and then waved them apart like little waves flowing away, stretching her arm towards the horizon.

"But they say *you* are well off, old man," she said familiarly. And with this affirmation, which was but a furtive question, she gave him a sudden and envious glance of quite astonishing sharpness. He walked heavily, swinging his bent shoulders.

"That's a lie, then," he said; "a fortune is not to be made out of mere good work."

Meanwhile, Pascale, who was evidently more taken by the attentions, the alertness, and the brave manner of Jules Prayou than by the rough advances of the weavers' sons of the Croix Rousse, spoke to him as though she wished to thank him for his confidence:

"The hospital? I had thoughts at one time of being a Sister of Saint Vincent de Paul."

"What a strange idea!"

"Why?" she asked innocently. "It would be a good thing to give one's life to the sick. It is work well worth doing. But it wants more strength than I have, and more courage. I have such a horror of blood—I cannot get over it."

"Ah, yes?"

"I can't bear to see a wound, nor even to hear about it, without turning faint. Can you?"

A laugh was his answer.

She proceeded: "That is why I chose a teaching Order."

"Oh, then you are a kind of bigot, are you?"

Jules Prayou took two or three steps forward, and turned to look at her, studying her with an

insistence which she took for interest. Had she
been able to read his look, until that moment
ingratiating, she would have seen it suddenly turn
hard, like a stone stripped of its moss. For some
minutes he ceased to take any notice of Pascale,
and even walked on a little before her. They
were passing along the edge of the wide cattle
market, and Jules Prayou, recognising here and
there, about the market or at the neighbouring
windows, young butchers or drovers of his acquaintance, of Provence or from the Cevennes,
greeted them with a wave of his thick and fleshy
hand. He called out words, besides, that Pascale
did not understand. It amused her to watch the
drama of head, eyebrows, eyelids, fingers, in this
young man, who seemed to know everybody. A
wide boulevard ran across the road. The wind
grew tempestuous. It raised the dust in deep
wreaths and tossed it against the small trees
planted in the aisles of the avenue. But the
brilliance of the sky was untroubled, and looked
immutable. This was the South—the sculpture
of desiccated earth under the blue. To the right
stood the Magne Tower, a golden and rosy prow
above the pine-garden of the fountain, steadfast
in the mistral wind.

They crossed the boulevard and reached the
Cadereau, the torrent that runs by Nîmes, separating the southern town from that other part
which rises by hillocks and hills towards the table-
land of the Cevennes. There lived the Prayous.

"A hundred steps more," said Jules, "and we
shall drink a glass of *carthagène* to lay the dust.

Have you never tasted *carthagène*, Mademoiselle
Pascale?"

"I never have, indeed."

"It's the new wine—the must, just as it comes
out of the wine-press, with a glass of brandy
thrown in. It's a treat—wait and see."

"Oh, this is country," cried Pascale, "and
houses—just an avenue of country houses. This
is where you live? It is very pretty."

"It is called Montauri, at your service."

The golden eyes welcomed with a youthful joy
the image of the charming hill covered with
orchards and olive trees, very slightly green, a
smoke of thin foliage scattered over the ground,
with white houses, near which stood erect the
dark shapes of cypress and stone pine.

The two couples followed the torrent for a few
moments, passed the tank for washing by the
roadside, and turning once to the right by a
bridge across the Cadereau, entered a single road,
a kind of sketch of a future suburb, crossed by
three little lanes, and climbing uphill between
wide cultivated lands full of olive trees. At two-
thirds of the length of the unfinished road, which
ended in a hedge, and just beyond the second
transverse lane, on the left, Jules Prayou pushed
open a door.

"Come in, Mademoiselle; come in, Monsieur
Mouvand. It is not a palace; but in ten years'
time, instead of this shed, I shall have my pretty
little country house on the hill."

"He seems full of enterprise," said the weaver
to the widow Prayou.

"Like his father, and more. Perhaps a little too much of that," she said in a low voice, showing her cousin in. "What he says I have to swear to."

"That's not so well."

She stopped him on the threshold. "And when he is in a rage with me, it's a terror to the neighbourhood. And strong too!"

She accompanied her last words with a grimace of admiration; and the weaver entered the door on the left of the passage separating the two rooms of the cottage. On the table in the middle, which was covered with a white oil-cloth bound with black, were placed four claret glasses full of *carthagène*. A provençal sideboard of light-coloured wood, fitted with iron and containing the plates and dishes, gave the place its character as a dining-room for great occasions. The bed filled a large space to the right of the window.

"Jules' place is at the end of the garden," added the woman, showing through the window a little house of two floors. "There he lives, like a prince. He is to give you your lodging to-night."

Tired with the journey, keen of appetite because of the cold, and pleased with the novelty of Nîmes, Adolphe Mouvand did honour to the local popular drink, and to the dinner prepared by the widow. Afterwards Pascale and her father were conducted to the little building at the end of the garden enclosure, where Jules Prayou had his usual dwelling. The father slept on the ground floor, next to a lumber room that served

as a lobby, and the girl had the little garret above,
where the widow had arranged a bed. Jules
Prayou was to sleep, apparently, in some corner of
the cottage in which his mother lived; they saw
no more of him until ten o'clock the next morning.

When she awoke, Pascale had the surprise of
a town girl who likes the country by a sense of
contrast and of privation, and who fancies that
she brings something of it into the town, after a
Sunday walk, when she carries a little scrap of
hawthorn or of lilac between her teeth. Through
her uncurtained window Pascale saw the heights
of Montauri, and in the foreground a wide piece
of waste land, upon which opened the yards and
gardens of the neighbours, a space of unequal
grass, interrupted by hollows that looked like
old chalk-pits, and sprinkled with unused stones
and clumps of thistle and other plants of hardy
stalks, discoloured by the winter, on which women
dried their household cloths. The pasture belonged to the Prayous, being the remainder of the
land bought by the father, who had built upon it
three small houses, his own and those that flanked
it. Beyond, the pale olive orchards clouded the
hills, enclosed in low terrace walls, and distinct
among those clouds rose thin almond trees, tufts
of laurels, of pines, of pomegranate trees, of oaks
gathered about the country houses, with a general
air of southern carelessness. Nothing was very
straight or neat or orderly.

Above all—and Pascale's fancy, easily charmed
by the sense of repose and sweetness, rested there
—the lovely sky enveloped in light the cultivation

garlanded with trees, and looked more limpid than ever. She could see great distances, and could distinguish the leafless branches which the far hill turned to the warmer south. There was gold and blue and fairness in the sunward sky, in place of the lurid mists of that familiar smoke of Lyons which was always so harsh to her lungs and so cold to her heart. Yes, the light was brighter to-day than yesterday. Pascale opened her window; the mistral at last was still, but the air was fresh. A flock of linnets, newcomers from the north, fluttered from orchard to orchard, a gay company full of small cries and flashing in the golden sun.

It was such a holiday as Adolphe Mouvand had longed for many a time. He was satisfied. The little party went out somewhat late in the morning, having waited for Jules, who came in late. The young man was out, "with friends, about some business," explained the widow. He came at last, his felt hat pushed back, a sprig of mimosa in his buttonhole, a red tie, and an airy greeting for all. He said, apart to the weaver, who stood in the street blinking in the brilliant sun with the look of an old dazzled, bearded owl:

"I can't say I am sorry to have kept you waiting, old man. I did a jolly bit of smuggling business last night."

"Smuggling?" said Mouvand quietly. "That is what I never did, my boy."

"Oh, but here——," replied Prayou; and his sinuous lips parted in a smile that was silent, quick, and contemptuous. Then, perceiving that the old fellow was waiting for some explanation——

"In this town," he said, "a man who is not afraid, who looks out for himself and has friends, may make a fortune with alcohol. Well, Mademoiselle, let us go on."

They saw everything that the usual excursionist sees, and in the self-same way, without a pause, without any means of associating a single historical or artistic interest to what they saw, with the same remarks: "Yes, that is beautiful. It's as good as anything in Lyons," applied to the imitation jewellery in the shops, to the Roman Maison Carrée, to the Law Courts, to the Pradier fountain, to the Roman amphitheatre, and to the churches, every one of which they entered to please Pascale. She had a manner of her own in kneeling, simply, naturally, without jerks, her reverent face to the altar, while the widow Prayou made twists and turns as she genuflected, and Jules remained standing. Then she listened to his wordy explanations. He was entirely ignorant, but he talked better than any man of Lyons. He was full of attentions, and the party had to enter a shop of "souvenirs" to choose something for Pascale—a silver cross, picture postcards, an album, a pair of scissors. "In a few days," remonstrated Pascale, in a low voice—she did not wish to remind her father of the approaching date of their parting—"I shall not be able to keep anything except perhaps the scissors. The silver cross is too pretty for me."

"Take it all the same," said Jules Prayou.

"When I make money I don't often spend it on crosses."

They were all dusty, tired, and in good spirits. When they had dined—late in the afternoon, in a little restaurant outside the town on the first slope of the Rhone hills, where Jules had an open account—they walked back to Montauri by stony roads between walls that were overtopped now and again by almond trees, pines, or cypresses, or even, despite the wintry month, by climbing roses still in flower. Pascale, the least weary of the four, cried: "Never before have I breathed so easily. It is four o'clock," she added, "and as bright as Lyons at noon." At times they went in through open doorways or breaches in the walls to the terraced enclosures of the cultivated lands—little properties of thirty olive trees, a couple of mulberry trees, a thirsty almond tree, and in the midst the little country house peculiar to Nîmes—the *mazet*—whither it is the family custom to go out on Sundays and rest in country shade. "We shall have one of our own in time," said the widow; "and a better one than those. A lot of stones, a shed, a few olive trees, and a little soil slipping away—they call that a *mazet*, but we shall do better with ours."

At the top of the hill of Montauri they met, at the old gateway of a villa, the caretaker and his wife, who knew the Prayous, and now invited them to come through the garden and rest themselves. The owners being away, and their consent by proxy being assumed, the party walked through an avenue, and Pascale and Jules sat together on the low wall that supported the garden terrace, rising from an olive orchard. Beyond, the ground rose again, and further still, between the beautiful lines of the descending hills, lay the whole city of Nîmes.

The town, which from this height looked flat, was tenderly coloured, rosy, almost violet, among its long and gentle hills, which clothed half of the horizon as with the folds of soft draperies. And the rose of the town and the green of the heights were tints so tender in the last great light of the sun that Pascale, unaccustomed to clear distances, felt their loveliness, and thought, "Here is no winter."

The colour of the plain too was full of harmonies of violet-grey—ploughed land, leafless woods, a region unfolding towards the south, low slopes that were mirrors for the sun and reflected his light into the hollows of the Rhone; and, further still, the sparkle of the waters of Aigues Mortes.

All these caresses of the light were of greater power and of sweeter influence because of the fore-ground foliage, through which they came like the glances of appealing eyes veiled by their lashes. Pascale, seated sideways on a wall, was receiving into her heart, at this time of keen emotion, many thoughts that had wandered in her world, but had not yet harboured within her. Jules Prayou, his feet swinging over the little orchard below, was not studying the landscape; he was marking the traces of the peasant's labour or the marauder's trespass among the olives. Adolphe Mouvand and the widow, not much moved by the beauty of the day, talked with the gardener about the harvest. Pascale, fully understanding the invitation to life and to joy implied in that view of the sunny city, said within her heart: "I give them all up, those delights, the thought of which disturbs me, those delights I have not known and shall never know. I am escaping them. I am taking refuge in the peace that is unlike them, that is better than they are, as I know at times when my soul is perfectly pure. I give them up—all the ambitions and all the enjoyments of which those streets are full, and all happiness that is not mingled with self-sacrifice. How many mothers of children are in those houses; and their children love them, and they are expecting their father home, or he has just come in, and they hold up the baby for a kiss. My children will not love me quite so much. But I shall have a great, great many, and God will make up for the fondness I shall miss." Her fresh lips moved with prayer. Jules Prayou ceased to stare about him; he looked, and looked ardently, at the charming face turned towards the city, and full of dreams in the light. He looked at the delicate head with its rays of fair hair against a background of laurels, at the neck, somewhat long and very white; at the drooping shoulders, over which his mother had thrown a little shawl of white wool, lifted regularly by each breath of the pure air. He would much have liked to laugh with the girl as he did with others, to have her attention, to pay her court; but he guessed that Pascale was at that moment very far from him in spirit, and he was seized with angry jealousy of the thing that absorbed her.

"I say, cousin," he said, raising his voice, "what a funny idea that is of yours—going into a convent."

"Why funny?" she said, still holding her face to the light. "To me it is exceedingly serious."

"Well, but for a pretty girl like you!"

"Oh!" she cried, and her laughter opened like a flower. "You think all nuns are plain, do you? I assure you some of them are lovely. You don't know much about such things, I suspect, cousin."

"Upon my word, one would think you were afraid of men."

She turned to him, and felt at last the dubious fire of the look that played upon her. She rose to her feet.

"I am not bound to tell you why I am to be a nun. My reasons are private, and no one's business but my own."

For the second time she had occasion to note the violence of what is called the southern temperament, but is only human instinct uncontrolled and unashamed. Jules Prayou flung her an insult, and leapt from the wall into the olive-ground at his feet. For some few minutes she watched him amongst the trees, striding excitedly, his hands in his pockets, turning on her now and again a face pallid with anger.

Pascale called him, thinking this was some kind of joke:

"Cousin! Come back!"

"Why, why, where's he going?" cried his

mother, running up. "You've been vexing him? What about?"

"I vexing him? I told him that my reasons for going into the convent were my business—that was all."

The woman shook her head; and as the slight and active figure of her son passed out of sight beyond a further wall, over which he vaulted with little respect for the owner of the garden or for the gardener, she said very gravely:

"Anyway, when he comes back, please be careful; don't annoy him again, be nice to him."

"If I am not to scold him, then will you?"

"You don't know him. He might——"

She did not finish her sentence, but suddenly added:

"He is terrible."

The three walked down the road of Saint Césaire, hoping to meet Jules Prayou, who had taken that direction across the orchards. But they could not see him. After half an hour's silence, and as they drew near the slaughter-house buildings in the gathering twilight, Adolphe Mouvand said, twisting his beard, and turning to the widow:

"You are not training that boy of yours. He is the master. Take care!"

The woman only laughed.

It was almost dark when they entered the cottage at Montauri. It was less cold than on the mistral evening, but Madame Prayou lighted a fire in her room and fed it during the evening with twigs of oak to which clung still their with-

ered leaves, and of which she had a store under
a shed. As she cherished illusory ideas in regard
to the wealth of her guests, and as the absence
of her son freed her from her habitual uneasiness
under his watchful eyes, she grew expansive.
She talked over the family history with Adolphe
Mouvand, who liked this gossip of the past; she
became affectionate to Pascale, and even made
some demonstration of a tendency to piety. She
again and again recommended her "intentions"
to the prayer of the future novice. She also asked
her to boil the water for the "grog." And leaning
back idly in her chair she sighed, "It *is* nice to
have a little help." Pascale, believing that in her
she had found something of that maternal tenderness of which she had so early been deprived,
allowed herself to be embraced and kissed, and
was moved, and proffered her own young, in-
genuous, and eager affection to this woman who
called her "my child," and used, as she spoke the
words, a warmth of voice, a naturally dramatic
mimicry in which her whole southern body took
part in confederacy with her words, filling with
sweet gratitude this daughter of the more north-
ern Lyons. The last hours spent thus in home
life—for Adolphe Mouvand could not further pro-
long his holiday—made a stronger impression on
Pascale's mind, and even on her father's, than
the pleasant journey had done. "A good woman,
that," said the weaver at night, as he crossed to
his own bedroom. "She talks too fast for me;
she doesn't bring up her boy properly; but she's
a kind soul, this cousin of ours."

On the following morning, half an hour before their departure, Jules Prayou arrived, eager, attentive, smiling as at their first meeting. He begged Pascale, in a tone of jest, to forget and forgive his hastiness of the previous evening; he asked permission to kiss her; he volunteered to carry the valise to the station; he promised, with a gesture towards the north, to visit his cousin some day, wherever her religious superiors might place her; and when the train drew away, and she saw these two new-found relatives, who multiplied their *au revoirs*, waving their hands—hands full of language—Pascale said to her father:

"I am glad we came."

He was so too; but what had made him glad was that during those two days he had not heard his own heart rehearsing constantly the hour, the day, the moment.

The last ten days had come. By tacit consent Pascale and her father spoke no more of their imminent separation. He had promised himself to be brave "so as to gain merit," as he said in his simple theology. She took pains to be sweet to him so as to thank him. And she succeeded; she made herself doubly dear. For the weaver and for his daughter those days were full of the joy of companionship, a joy to which both gave utterance, to which they recurred, willing to make it stronger since it was to be short, and as the secret underpain of separation grew more instant. When father and daughter looked at one another each perceived the ineffaceable date in the other's eyes, and smiled "I do not see it." Pascale was gay for his sake, and made him believe her. She wished to leave him the memory of a Pascale who had been happy to the end. One morning she had laid out on the top of her chest of drawers the two summer dresses she possessed, the one very poor and much worn, a woollen dress in two shades of grey, the other a cotton dress, almost elegant, white with violet flowers, and ruffled at the wrists and throat. Had she wished to look at them again, to touch them, to give them away? Her father who, since the visit to Nîmes, was wont often to leave his loom for a little chat in her room or in the kitchen, came upon Pascale as she was folding the sleeves, and doubling them across the bodices, and gathering up the folds of the skirts. He drew back for an instant. Pascale saw, and said quickly, "It wants ironing, you see, and I'm not clever at gauffering. I shall get the workwoman to do it." He calculated; the workwoman would take four or five days; he pressed his lips together under his moustache, did not say why he had come, and turned away. Innumerable farewells, perpetual farewells, dumb farewells! They filled those hours for Pascale. When she touched anything in this little home, she said inwardly, "I shall never touch it again." She put her silver thimble away in a drawer, and said, "I shall never use it again." She took her father's arm as though for a mere walk in the neighbouring districts of the city, and looked with a passionate interest at the houses, the signs, the little side-alleys towards the Rhone and the park of the Tete d'Or. She took leave thus of many

and many who did not know it. As she had not
announced her purpose, many dwellers in those
streets were surprised at her lingering looks, and
at her shaking hands with them when they were
but passing in a hurry, or as they stood on their
door-steps. "She has got time on her hands,
that Pascale Mouvand," they said. No, she was
detaining something of the youth with which she
must finally part. She could not say to them,
"You will not see me again. You stout milk-
woman, who used to think me a pretty child, and
told me so by filling my jug a little fuller than the
rest; bustling, married neighbours, who compared
your own girlhood with mine; poor invalid behind
that window, who always watched me pass until
the glass was dim with your breath; fountain,
where the little boys out of school make the water
squirt; people out walking on Sunday, who don't
know that next Sunday there will be a girl the
less; hearers of daily early Mass, who will never
have me near you again, farewell to all, good-bye!
Good-bye to the eyes, the voices, the hearts, the
words, the cries, my pleasures, my pains, my
trouble and my weakness. It is hard to leave
you all!"

She renewed her strength in the single-hearted
meditation wherein her resolution had first been
formed, and she renewed it also in the courage
of her father. For she knew that she could not
walk without an example, a rail to guide her
hand. The weaver had made of the matter as
it were a point of honour between himself and
his God. "We won't give way," he said, "I

have principles; have I or have I not? Well,
I don't intend to flinch because I have to suffer
for my principles. Nor will I let my mates who
don't think as I do say that I am a bigot just as
long as it costs me no trouble. They shall see
whether or not I am one of the men of Saint
Irénée, from father to son Christians and first
class silk-weavers. And then—if there were
nothing else—I owe it to God for my sins. I gave
Him back my Pascale as I would my blood, drop
by drop."

And not for a moment had he flinched; he
had turned to all, and especially to his daughter,
that customary silent front which from time to
time was changed by an access of facile good
humour. If he wept within, there was nothing
to show it. Pascale sometimes thought, "His
nature is happier than mine." At any rate it
was more robust.

During the two last days they walked out
often, her hand on his arm, and they visited
some of their neighbours. The weather had
grown mild; three hours of moist, warm sunshine
between the morning mist and the evening fog.
They gave no reason for those ceremonial visits,
and those on whom they called were somewhat
surprised; but why speak yet? That surprise
would not be for long.

On the evening before Pascale's going, Adolphe
Mouvand and his daughter made their prayer
together. Pascale led, and her father made the
responses; and the man's voice was unsteady
because he had heard the child's, the voice that

was to sound no more in his house. Their evening kiss was long, their embrace was close.

The morning rose with an almost pure sky, the Christmas morning. Neither had courage enough for a first greeting. When he was ready, Aholphe Mouvand opened the door on the staircase and called, "Pascale." She came, carrying in her hand a bag of brown cloth in which she had folded six chemises and nightgowns and four pairs of black stockings, all the outfit and all the dowry wherewith she was to enter St. Hildegarde's. When her father appeared, he made haste to go down, for grief had caught his throat, and he could not trust himself to stand on the threshold. Pascale went down a step, pale and erect, but suddenly, as though she had forgotten something, she put her bag down and fled back into her room. She had, however, forgotten nothing. She ran into her little room, closed the door behind her, looked one last time round the four bare and faded walls, and one by one tenderly kissed them. Then she went out quickly, having said farewell to all her past.

Adolphe Mouvand was at the foot of the stairs. He did not turn when he heard behind him a woman's stifled weeping. Together, looking before them, they set forth. Now and then the weaver passed his hand over his beard fringed with frost. The neighbours hardly noted how strangely grave looked "those Mouvands," or the small care they took of their footing on the hill on that frosty morning. Soon they were two without a name, two without a history, in the great city then awaking. They spoke few words, and those such as express none of the tenderness they imply.

"Not cold, are you?" "Take care of the gutter —it's frozen!" And once the weaver said, "We'll take this way, it's rather longer round," and his face was twisted with a grimace of pain controlled. They might not much delay, for Pascale had promised to be, before eight o'clock, in the parlour of a school the Sisters kept at La Guillotière. Twice again did Mouvand speak. As they entered that quarter of the town he stopped Pascale on the quay by the Rhone, and said to her in his gruff voice, but in the tone of a child, "Pascale, will you come back home again?"

She, with her eyes before her, whispered "No, no," and went on.

Her father followed her. When he saw before him the Place de l'Abondance, open and empty and so quickly to be crossed, he said again, like a beggar losing hope for alms, "Will you come back home, Pascale?" She did not answer, perhaps she did not hear. He had said to her the night before, "I shall not see the Superior. I shall take you just to the door as I used to do when you were a child."

The school had a triangular façade to the street, and bore a cross. Pascale rang quickly, so as to make her act final. Then, hearing the tinkle of the little worn bell as she stood on the step on the level of her father standing on the pavement, she turned to him, and wept bitterly on his neck.

"I do love you, father," she said. "I shall love you as long as I live." She drew away, she looked at him with her ardent eyes that were heavy with tears, as though to fix the image of this dear one. With the action of a mother she laid the large and hairy head upon her breast, and slowly kissed the brow. The door was open. A young portress had said gaily, "Why, it's our new Sister," and then had stopped abruptly, struck silent by pity. Pascale whispered closely, while her father, bewildered, closed his eyes.

"I thank you for being so generous. I do love you, father. Good-bye, good-bye." She smiled to the Sister, went up two steps, and the door shut between the father and the child.

Mouvand sat down on the step and wept without control.

*   *   *   *   *   *

Two years went by while Pascale made her novitiate at the Mother-House of Clermont-Ferrand. The weaver grew accustomed to the absence of his child, at any rate there was no one in the district of the Croix Rousse who could say that he had not become used to it. For a week there was much talk of Pascale's vocation and departure; also of the weaver's taking an apprentice. But the apprentice did not live in the house. He came in the morning, and at whatever hour this was, he never failed to see the great shoulders of his master bent at the loom. Never had Mouvand worked so hard. Never had he grown old so fast; his bass voice grew hollow, and every wrinkle became a furrow. When the neighbours jested with him about his little nun,

he answered: "As there are girls for pleasure,
there have to be girls for prayer—that's how I
look at it."

When he heard, at the end of December, 1899,
that Pascale was to be sent, as auxiliary teacher,
to the school in the Place Saint Pontique, he was
happy; for she might never have returned to
Lyons at all. He said to the apprentice, a beard-
less youth as pale as a lamp forgotten and left
alight in broad day: "I shall have a good Sunday,
Joannès, I am going to see my girl at Saint
Pontique." And he thought: "How pretty she
will be, just twenty, in her nun's dress." And he
was right. In the little white parlour, when he
had kissed her with all his heart, he looked at her.
He sat in his chair, and she in one opposite, and he
conned her, feature by feature.

"Your eyes are still like flowers, yellow, like
the middle part of a daisy."

She laughed as she used to do, or even in a
fresher and clearer voice, for teaching had not
yet worn it.

"But your hair is gone, and I liked it so.   No—
there is a little bit, just by your ear."

"It will come out so."

"It's golden. All the gold we had at home.
You ought to have left me a lock. But you are
rosier, your cheeks and your mouth too."

"Dad, we don't talk of things of that kind."

"It's only your father, Pascale, and it has been
two years."

Ah, the sweet first five minutes! After that
they tried to talk easily. She spoke to him about

her companions, to him strangers; about Clermont-
Ferrand, where he had never been; about the
method and course of teaching in the school, for
which he cared nothing. She good-naturedly
asked him questions about the old district, about
business. By this time many things had grown
dim in the mind of Pascale: many details were
quite effaced, many figures had vanished; the
little novelties about the house or the street—she
had not seen them. Mouvand was well aware that
though she made some effort to imagine certain
new streets that he tried to describe, and the new
loom and the pattern of the new paper he had put
up "to make the room look warmer," she hardly
succeeded, and, besides that, it was her kindness
that was concerned, and not her life. He understood that they had no share together in the
house, or the street, or the work; that the one
thing belonging to them both was past, and that
they would never have another holiday together
except on the yonder side of the grave. Mouvand
felt that his sacrifice was not yet complete. He
asked:

"Are you happy, Pascale?"

"Quite happy."

"As you used to be?"

She was loth to answer, "Much happier"; she
nodded. Yes, he knew she was happy, he hardly
understood how—without him, far from him—
but the fact was there. He arose, before the
allotted hour of recreation was over. He touched
caressingly with his finger the white frontlet that
covered the fair hair, and the black veil, and the

hands of his child. He said, "I shall come again. It's always on Sunday, isn't it, that I can see you?"

But several months went by before he came again. His friends, the bowl-players, noticed that he had less power in throwing and that his bowl was often short. The wine that followed the game hardly cheered him whom it used to make joyful. He had not given up his visits to Pascale, but they were few and brief. His robust faith had grown yet stronger in solitude; he was not melancholy, but he no longer loved life. He said in his prayers: "I am old, I am common, I am quite alone and forsaken. It is not possible for anyone to love me again, except God only. God only! Glory! Alleluia! My soul is half saved." Since his child had taken the veil he always lifted his hat to nuns in the street, but he avoided speaking to them, because of the little girl of whom they too much reminded him. He had grown very emotional. Probably he had been so all his life, but if so, it was within, after the manner of the strong, out of sight of the effeminate and the curious. Now that he was a weaker man, and unable to work more than eight hours a day, his nerves had "got," as he said, "the upper hand," and he felt himself to be subject to sensibilities, which no one had before suspected to be lurking in him. More regularly than ever before he attended the meetings of the Hospitallers, and on Sundays, with his brothers of that Order, he went his round of the wards of fever-beds to which he was appointed. He visited

his patients, combed and cut their hair, and
shaved them, lifted them, talked with them, meeting, in the course of this ministration, men of his
mind and of his spirit. Formerly, he had visited
the sick and tended them in their own homes as
well, but this he could do no longer.

One morning towards the end of the summer,
as he was standing in his white-pouched apron,
deftly shaving the cheeks of a patient, one of
the Hospital nursing Sisters passed the foot of the
bed and said to him: "Monsieur Mouvand, your
chief wants you in the next room."

She went on, with her light and noiseless foot.
Her white linen—cap, frontlet, gorget and collar—
vanished beyond a door and took with it a flash
of white light.

The weaver had laid his left hand, holding the
shaving cloth, upon the sick man's bed; his
other hand held the razor; he remained leaning
aside, his head forward like a dog pointing. It
was only after a full minute that he became
again conscious of what he was about to do, and
recovered himself. Then he made haste to
"finish his customer," put his shaving things into
his pouch again, and went out into the hall,
where the "conductor" of his division of Hospitallers waited to ask a question. When he had
replied, he began to take off the apron of his
amateur calling.

"You look much worse than a great many of
our patients, Mouvand. You had better take a
little turn outside, it would pull you together,"
said his chief.

The weaver's head shook as it often did before he spoke. Then he said:

"I shall not come again."

"Not till next time!"

"No, never."

"You feel worn out?"

"Yes, I feel about done. I'm out of it. Please tell the other fellows I'm not fit for work. But there's another reason—I can't bear to see the Sister—the one who went through just now. She is too much like my daughter Pascale. Good-bye."

Nor did he enter the hospital again. Nor was he seen again on Sundays except at church, and on the Boulevard of the Croix Rousse at bowls. His friends sometimes threw the little bowl to a shorter distance, or, when his back was turned, pushed his own nearer, so that he might have the pleasure of winning.

In the spring of 1902 he was absorbed in an important piece of work—the weaving of a magnificent white silk, for the manufacture of which he had been chosen among several hundred workmen, by the head of the famous Lyons house of Talier-Décapy. He worked at this with extreme care, washing his hands ten times a day. It was a thick and supple silk, white as snow, sprinkled with little wreaths of silver foliage. He had both pleasure and pride in weaving this robe of light. On the 16th of May, which is the eve of St. Pascal, he came home from a visit to his child, and had two delights hidden in his heart: he had found Pascale looking well, and she had said to him,

"I am coming round to see you, I am coming to beg. The house at Clermont-Ferrand is full of evicted Sisters, and cannot give us any help. So we want some hundreds of francs for our own bread until the end of the year."

"Some hundreds of francs, forsooth! I can only give you a little—still, come all the same."

What a dream to cherish! Pascale again at the Croix Rousse! Pascale going up the Grande Côte, Pascale in the street below with her blue gown and her veil! Pascale's voice in the room from which it had so long kept away old age! Pascale's eyes reflecting the things of the house and her father's image, as when she used to come behind him at his loom, and say, "Well, no kissing this morning, Dad, I suppose?"

The second delight, which did but attend the first, was in the weaver's heart as he walked home along the Saône in the sweet weather, his hands in his pockets, and felt the summer wind, fresh only when it is high. And on the quay was a little greenery, enough to give a factory workman a sense of the country, and he enjoyed and loved the foliage and the breeze.

Mouvand walked quickly that day. He was heated when he sat down before his loom and lifted the paper covering his silk. With more spirit than usual his foot pressed the pedal, his left hand pushed the leaf, and his right hand threw the shuttle. He worked for more than an hour, and the light was fine in the workshop. The apprentice had stopped to rest three times. Mouvand, excited by the beauty of the material

in his hands and the splendour of the tissue in
his loom, sat intent with his shoulders bowed
and his rough head covered by the cap with
ears which he usually wore at work. The sound
of the bell did not stop him, nor did the entrance
of an employé of the factory, who was taking
an Italian client round the works. This visitor,
with a thin southern face and pointed beard, drew
near the weaver, looked at him closely for a
moment, studied his work, and touching his
shoulder, said:

"Excellent!"

Mouvand stopped the shuttle at the point
where the stretched threads of the "chain" made,
as it were, long rays from the woven light of
the lustrous silk. He even lifted a finger to
his cap.

"I have brought to your workshop, Monsieur
Mouvand," said the employé, "the greatest of
all exporters of Italian silk. Now, sir, you can
judge of the good work of our Lyons weavers;
and here is one of the best."

"And the last," said Mouvand in his gruff
voice. "No cheap silk, no ribbon in this workshop!"

The Italian was full of genuine admiration.
He touched the silk and smiled at it; he would
have liked to speak to it.

"You are an artist," he said, "and you are
making a masterpiece. Is it for a ball-dress?"

The old weaver, well pleased to be so praised
in the presence of Joannès, his apprentice, but
still better pleased at an acknowledgment of his

merit deserved by so many years of the past, lifted his cap as he proclaimed:

"Court-dress for the Coronation of the King of England."

The loud words resounded down the faded walls and windows, embrowned with winter smoke. It was the voice of the pride of ancestors, creators of the Lyons industry; it was the voice of all the emotion of a secluded and laborious life, unenvious of the riches it produced.

When the two visitors were gone, Mouvand, in the same high tone, addressed his apprentice who, having closed the door, was taking, in good spirits, his seat again.

"Take notice, Joannès. You are in the workshop of an artist. An artist; and I think I was right, mind you, when I said the last one!"

He worked on till night, so as to finish the piece if possible. The visit had greatly moved him, and this was the third joy of the day.

On the following morning, at seven, when Joannès entered the workshop, he found his master seated at the loom, with his arms folded on the silk, which was unfinished by about a quarter of a yard. Adolphe Mouvand was dead.

*　　*　　*　　*　　*　　*

Pascale's grief over this death did much to shake her health, long tried by overwork and by the lack of air and exercise. Her companions abounded in attentions, services, tender words, reverent and considerate silence. They were all quick at guessing, all—whether daughters of the

farm, the workshop, or the office—accustomed to
meditate on that Passion of the Master which is a
clue to all other griefs. Pascale found amongst
them the counsel and the support she needed.
She had her own battle to fight, but she had help
from her fellows. She was adored by the school-
children, who were quite aware of her weakness,
and read in the tender sweep of her eyelashes when
she answered their "Good morning," in the caress-
ing grasp of her hand, in the contraction of her
face when she heard of an accident or saw a wound,
the dominance of affection and of emotion in the
young heart of their teacher. The youngest ran
to her when they saw her in the courtyard or in the
passages; some of them kissed her hands, clinging
to her motherly young skirt; and during the long
play-time of holiday afternoons, when Sister
Pascale was in charge, the eldest girls stood by her
and entrusted her with avowals of all that most
nearly touched their hearts—trials in regard to
dress and to lovers. She did not love to hear these
things, which threatened her with the unquiet
things of life. She answered, laughing:

"But why do you tell me, my dears? I have
no experience; I can't tell you what I should have
done in your place, when I was a weaver's daughter in the Croix Rousse, for I don't know." What
she did love was the Office said at the end of the
day by the Sisters together, their quiet recreation,
their evening prayer: that peace which was still
vibrating with the life and feeling of the day, and
full of the consciousness of the watchful love of
those who cherished her—a love in arms for her

against the temptations or terrors of the night.
She loved the Great Silence of the Rule, which
lasted until morning Mass was over. What a
refreshing and renewing of the soul was there!
"Grace comes down in the Silence," said Pascale.
She was not mystical, but she had fervent im-
pulses of devotion, movements of a soul that
knows the way, and though it cannot follow it all
by continuous flight, can leap and flutter as well
as run, and does not go astray. She was very
punctual, even to scruple, in the observance of the
Rule. She loved the children she taught—loving
the prettiest best, as at first—and her love grew
with the sense of duty fulfilled. She—beloved
by four saintly women—might well be on the way
to become a saint like them.

Therefore the news that the community was
in danger troubled the very depths of Pascale's
being. All night long the past went by in the
young nun's heart; she travelled again her old
road, and she tried in vain, and in terror, to guess
at the future which was like the night, menacing,
pressing, perilous. She rose all undone with
weariness.

III.

VIA DOLOROSA.

TUESDAY morning was wearing on. In the bright light the school-children, prisoners, like wasps in a hot-house, were beginning to grow languid. Thirty little girls of six to eight years old who were writing copies, with bent backs, often lifted their eyes towards their mistress. Pascale was dictating:

"A voice was heard in Rama. Rachael weeping for her children and will not be comforted, because they are not."

Poor tender voice, which the children heard, for they were used to its weakness.

"Have you understood the dictation?" she said. "Read it over to yourselves. I will make the corrections later. Mélie, come up to me."

A child rose, with a single impetus of her agile body, and drew near to the teacher's desk. She was red-haired, with hard and quick blue eyes, wide mouth, sharp teeth, a little wolfish head above a small figure clad in a grey woollen frock; the eldest pupil in the class (ten years old) and the most inattentive. She stood on the step of the mistress's desk, her bold eyes on the tired eyes of Sister Pascale. The mistress faced the window, and the child was in shadow. Most of the other pupils stopped to listen; some few read over their dictation.

In a low tone Sister Pascale said:

"My little girl, I am obliged to speak to you again."

Mélie made a grievously disrespectful movement of the shoulders.

"What for? I did my writing, the same as the others."

"That is not what I mean."

"I didn't talk."

"No, that's true."

"What is it then?"

"You did not come to Mass the day before yesterday."

The child frowned, looking askance at her companions, who uplifted their noses and tittered at seeing that Mélie was in trouble again—Mélie the idle, the unruly and perverse.

Mélic had her mind's eye fixed afar upon the hovel that was her dwelling, and she said nothing.

Sister Pascale leaned over her and said very softly:

"Do you wish to make me unhappy, my child?"

"That I don't."

And for a moment the little wild face fronted the face of Pascale. The child was gloomy still, and angry, but now because she was misunderstood, and because this Sister Pascale did not see how much a turbulent child loved her and wanted to kiss her before all the school. The ardent reproach of those childish eyes was perceptible enough to Pascale, whose own expression relaxed somewhat as the child said:

"I'm going to tell you—I won't tell anybody else, though—I couldn't come."

"Tell me why."

"Saturday evening, father and mother both came in .all—anyhow, I had to put them both to bed. They made a noise all night long; so in the morning I was asleep."

Pascale's hand lay, as though giving absolution, on the rough head of Mélie. The child lifted herself on tiptoe so as the better to meet that caress— she, the beaten one, the worse than motherless, the despised.

"Go then," said Sister Pascale—and as she said it, a thought from the once familiar life of the streets struck her. "They won't be drinking every Saturday I hope, will they? So you'll come next Sunday, and the other Sundays?"

She stopped abruptly. What was she saying? Next Sunday? the other Sundays? Two tears hung on the lashes of her childish eyes.

Mélie went back to her place, saying: "Sister Pascale is unhappy. She couldn't smile."

The other children had not heard, but they had looked. "What did she say? Crying, is she? What is she crying for? Had you told a lie? Is she unhappy? Why? Did she tell you?" The little girls were restless in the heat. Sister Pascale was trying to resume her school-mistress voice: "We will now correct the dictation—." She was not released until the bell sounded for the play-hour. Then she hurried to find the Superior, so as to hear something more of the fate of the community.

"Sister Pascale," said Sister Justine, meeting her in the corridor, "you will take charge of the luncheon of the day-boarders. What a Lenten face you have, my child! Why, what a reed you are!"

Pascale, during the play-hour, tried to join in the games, as her duty was; to be gay and to be obedient. But she felt within her a burden of tears. Around her the little girls ran and skipped with a hum of summer flies. The young mistress played, and was beaten every time. She caught sight, at intervals, of Sister Léonide, in a hurry as usual, trotting, laughing with her toothless mouth to the little girls who shouted to her across the playground; or of Sister Edwige, who was standing very still and very good, in her blue gown, in the recess of one of the windows, correcting a sheaf of exercises.

At half past four—the "parents' hour"—the four women met, the cook-Sister being in the kitchen. They were together as the front door closed upon the last child.

"Well?" said the anxious voice of Pascale. "What have you settled, Mother? What is to become of us? Have you any plans? What have you done?"

The Superior, who delighted in these extra-school moments of life "in community," bowed her large face with its deep wrinkles in turn to the three in order of seniority. "Good day," she said, "my children. School is over, and we

can breathe again. What have I done? Well,
I have begun a letter."

"And then?"

"Then I shall finish it, and I shall send it to
the post to-night by Sister Léonide."

"And is that all?"

"I shall expect the answer of our Mother-
General, who will write by Thursday, I suppose, either to our Superior, Canon Le Suet, or
to me."

"And in the meantime?"

"The two days? We shall go on with the school
and with our prayers."

"But if——."

Sister Pascale hesitated, but as she was privi-
leged and was permitted some of the freedom of
speech she had brought with her from the Croix
Rousse, she added:

"If none of us say anything, what then?"

The steady eyes of Sister Justine rested on the
face of the questioner:

"It is only then, my little Pascale, that we
shall have to depend upon ourselves."

*　　　*　　　*　　　*　　　*　　　*

Two days later, immediately after the mid-
day dinner, which was cooked in twenty minutes
and eaten in fifteen, Sister Justine and the nun
who on special occasions bore the part of her companion—Sister Danielle—crossed Saint Pontique
and the Perrache railway station, and on the south
road took the tramcar, for they were pressed for
time and had far to go. Seated together, they

exchanged few words, covered by the noise of the wheels and of the rattling windows.

"Do you think the Canon has received orders?"

"I should think so, since nothing has come to me from Mother-General."

"He is sure to tell us to go to Clermont-Ferrand."

"It is most likely."

"We shall have to ask him about the trains, as we never travel and he does sometimes."

"Oh, Sister Léonide knows all about it. Fancy asking Monsieur le Supérieur such things as that! Sister Danielle, what are you thinking of?"

During some part of the journey they were silent, both thinking of Clermont-Ferrand. As the tramcar came in sight of the Pont de Tilsit, Sister Danielle said in a whisper:

"I shall see there several Sisters with whom I made my novitiate. I cannot help being glad of that. And yet how can they give shelter in the Mother-House to Sisters from every corner of France where schools have been closed? If our Order had missions in other countries—missions to the heathen—but as it is——."

They had crossed the Saône and reached their destination—the square and respectable house on the Quai Fulchiron, where dwelt Canon Le Suet.

This was an ecclesiastic who, clad in his cassock, looked as broad as he was tall and as thick as he was broad. And yet he was not precisely fat, and had considerable dignity in his bearing, some sweetness, and much ease—a well-mitigated zeal. His life was above reproach, and his con-

fidence in himself apparently unlimited. All the
priesthood of Lyons knew him. A priest of the
Concordat, as he essentially was, for him accord
with the State was the one thing needful. The
price of peace was never too great, peace being
beyond price; and even the honour of the religion
in which he sincerely believed might conceivably
be given in order to secure it. He had deep-set
eyes, thin hair somewhat long, thick brows and
a face that sometimes turned white under a
breath of unuttered apprehension. Abbé Le
Suet was an adviser to whom many applied in
trouble, but from whom few received comfort.
Those who sought him had often to leave his
presence taking little provision with them on
their homeward journey except such phrases as
they might have read for themselves in the news-
papers: "The times are very difficult. But with
goodwill things may be settled—goodwill on both
sides. The Catholic party is not entirely faultless.
You certainly have cause of complaint, and I feel
for you; but you should have foreseen this, and
done that, and thought of the other, etc., etc., in
good time; you understand me—in good time."
But precisely what he advised, or would in good
time have advised, neither those who had known
him for years nor those who knew him little could
easily tell. He had always blamed his friends, he
had always had his fears. His function had been
that of a discreet drag upon the hasty. His way
was to advise no action whatever "for the present." His mind worked most clearly and most
effectually among small local and ecclesiastical

affairs strictly of the past. On those subjects
he was profuse. His memory was inexhaustible.
He remembered the "unfortunate" phrases that
had escaped former *vicaires* before the Council—
that is, phrases of too "ultramontain" a character. No such phrases were recorded of any
speech of his. His almsgiving was normal. He
was supposed to be rich, but this word is altogether relative when a French priest is in question.
Some of his colleagues were dazzled by the comfortable appointments of his waiting-room, inasmuch as the chairs were covered with blue rep, and
the walls hung with old prints of sacred subjects
after one or other of the Poussins, and the room
contained, moreover, a vase of artificial flowers
(under glass), the offering of some community of
nuns, and a cuckoo clock from the Black Forest.
The owner of all this luxury was wont to repeat
the sermons of his earlier years, touching them
to life by means of exceedingly modern instances.
He had been appointed Honorary Canon in 1885.
His chances of a bishopric had been spoken of, but
were spoken of no longer. He might have been a
candidate, not through vanity merely, but by the
conviction that he would have been a good "ad-
ministrator"—a Bishop of business. He was, in
fact, a good layman, tonsured; he was orthodox,
of medium character, of mediocre intellect, always
incapable of falsehood, or treason, but now also
incapable of action, desiring peace in the midst
of war, a straggler playing the flute in the rear
of an army.

When Sister Justine rang the Canon's bell, the

servant, the clean, the cool, the aged Zoë, who looked somewhat like a police inspector, knew her at once, and said drily:

"I hardly know whether Monsieur le Supérieur can see you. I should be surprised, as he is leaving this afternoon."

"For Paris?" asked Sister Justine.

"No, he is going to Vichy."

She returned after five minutes.

"Come in; but don't stay long."

She showed the Sisters, with a motion of her shoulder, the door, which they had crossed more than once before, and retreated to her kitchen.

Almost immediately the priest appeared, from his own parlour, made no apology for receiving the nuns in the waiting-room, and took his seat in an armchair, saying:

"Let me hear what you wish to say."

Then he closed his eyes.

They had taken the two small chairs. The priest, leaning forward with his elbows on his knees, nodded slowly and made inarticulate sounds in parentheses to the narrative of Sister Justine, so as to prove to her that he was not slumbering.

"What is to be done, Monsieur le Supérieur?" she asked, at the end of her report. "We are warned that our school is to be closed on the day after to-morrow. Are we to make any resistance?"

"Certainly not," said the Canon, opening his mouth and eyes at once, and speaking in a tone of authority. "I am entirely opposed to anything of the kind. What about the Mother-House? Would you get that closed too?"

"No, Monsieur le Supérieur; we wish only to record our right. If there is no show of violence, if the convent is not attacked, how will the people know that it is not by our own wish that we are forsaking our work?"

The priest said:

"Do not let us provoke——"

"But, Monsieur le Supérieur, they are robbing us, they are turning us out of our own property, they are tearing our children from us, they are preventing our community life——"

"Excuse me, excuse me——"

"Well, our community life in Lyons, at any rate. We are to leave the school in two days, and to retire to the Mother-House."

"Who told you that?"

"Why, the police people. Where should we go if not there?"

"It is quite impossible," said the priest, adjusting his glasses and looking at the two women alternately. "It is quite out of the question for you to be received at the Mother-House. It is absolutely full."

The Sisters started. They said together:

"What, do you mean that we cannot go to Clermont?"

"I am advised," replied the priest, "by a letter from the Superior-General, who is in great distress—I was going to write to tell you before I left—that there is no room."

"But then?"

He lifted both hands, as though to say, "So it is."

"That means we must separate?"

He bowed.

"We must be secularised?"

He bowed again.

"Separate—Sister Danielle, Sister Edwige, Sister Pascale?"

"My dear daughter——"

"Give up our work, our teaching, go back into the world, lose all—all? You have not settled it? We may still telegraph to the Mother-House? They might——"

"I know what they might do, and it is very little indeed," broke in the Canon.

He opened a drawer, and took between his finger and thumb some coins wrapped in a piece of newspaper.

"Very little indeed. The Mother-House is poor, and three thousand nuns have now to be supported without return. I have been asked to hand to each of you forty francs. It is a little send off. A good lady has also provided, I hear, an outfit for the secularised Sisters. You will call on her on leaving the school, and she will supply you."

"And then where do we go?"

The Canon rose and made a melancholy grimace because of the embarrassment of the interview.

"Wherever you may find a—an opening. Circumstances have been too strong for us. I am truly sorry that I in vain foretold what was to happen. You must practise self-sacrifice. You must bow to the storm, and let it go by."

He was sincerely distressed at having to see before him these two unhappy women, white as their frontlets. Sister Justine paused for a moment, made up her mind not to resist him, and stammered: "Good-bye, Monsieur le Supérieur; we shall not forget your goodness. We beg you to remember us in your prayers."

Both the Sisters bowed respectfully and crossed his door again. At the street corner Sister Danielle said, without halting, as they went:

"*Passio Domini Nostri Jesu Christi.*" Her voice was firm, but thrilling with energy and indignation. She looked along the quay with its houses, she looked at the mass of the city, and in these she saw the world upon which she had just been cast back, which she had abjured, the world, which meant trouble, impurity, blasphemy, pride of dress, all that made against the peace of the spirit. Within her soul the virgin, the woman, the peasant protested, but she controlled that revolt, commanding all except the turbulent blood that rushed from her beautiful face to her suffering heart. Sister Justine was busy with thoughts about the thing to be done. Long, long ago she had formed her judgment of men, and had forgiven them beforehand whatever injustice, whatever unkindness, whatever insult, they might make her endure. In the street, from the moment of her first step, one resolution had been taken, and another was in her thoughts. The only sign of her distress was the greater than usual vigour and assurance of her aspect. The old nun marched quickly, eyes front, like a soldier.

"Where are we going?" asked Danielle.

"Why, to get advice," said the Superior with that short laugh which mingled so much good humour with her office and her authority. "For, indeed, it is hardly advice that we have just received."

"Our work is at an end," said Sister Danielle.

"But the Sisters are not at an end, dear child."

"And who now will advise us, Mother?"

"The saints. There are always saints, and now there is no one else."

Her companion knew then that they were on their way to the Abbé Monechal. At the end of the Place Bellecour Sister Justine turned to the left, and they walked to the foot of the heights of the Croix Rousse.

This priest lived in the over-populated quarter of the Torreaux, where, within smoky and leprous walls, a great number of silk merchants and manufacturers had their offices. In a house of business, with agents and workmen on the upper storeys, and in poor rooms, once roughly repaired and since then again stained and faded, he dwelt on a ground floor well fitted for the very poor. It was also well fitted for a priest, their friend. There was an approach of three steps to the front door, no bell, and the first room, unfurnished, with plastered walls, gave access to another, smaller, an alcove with no door, in which the priest set at night his camp bed, folded up by day. The whole of the mornings and a part of the afternoons he devoted here to his visitors—hunger, misery, grievance, discontent, destitution, vice, virtue in disguise, grief beyond consolation. The outer

room served for those who awaited their turn; in
the inner he received the confidences of his poor
clients. He had formed part of the body called
the higher clergy, but was now a free missionary,
himself in want by reason of that rare and splendid
cause of ruin—charity.

Sister Justine and Sister Danielle were not kept
waiting; there was no one in the "drawing-room."
Within, they saw, bent over the deal table, the
weary Abbé asleep. On his two folded arms
rested the bowed forehead, and nothing was to
be seen but two cassock sleeves, a broad un-
tonsured head with short white hair, and a back
breathing quietly. The two nuns waited respectfully at a few steps' distance from the table.
Other visitors might have made, with pretended
inadvertence, a little noise. These two, by un-
spoken consent, stood silent, and inwardly prayed
for the man who was resting under his burden of
work, and who was lonelier than they. His loneliness seemed to them the hardest of his griefs.
But there are mysterious bells within souls that
live and are fervent. A part of the being that
never sleeps, the watcher of the ship at anchor,
now roused the crew. The priest raised his head,
looked up, passed his hand over his eyelids and
said, without embarrassment: "I beg your pardon, Sisters. This does happen to me sometimes—I am growing old." His memory had not
yet given him the names of his visitors. But a
moment later he recalled them, and with a slight
bow he said:

"Sister Justine, I think? Sister Danielle?

Yes, pray sit down. On whose behalf are you here, dear children?"

But they stood, their hands in their sleeves. And in the convent dress, in the convent attitude, they almost resembled each other bearing as they did the mark of the self-same trouble. They looked like witnesses at the tribunal of God.

"We have a great misfortune to endure," said Sister Justine, "and we have come to ask you how we are to meet it."

Then she told the story of the last three days. The Abbé Monechal listened intently, his eyes lowered, his hands on the table. His bald brow with its wrinkled protuberances, his large, uneven nose; his wide jaw and hollow cheeks; the faded mouth, deeply marked at the corners with the fold of compassion, denoted at once the vigour and the weariness of the man. He was not yet old, but he was deeply worn. Hearing Sister Justine, he was thinking:

"More suffering for the poor. How the impious hate these friends of Christ! It is as His friends that they are driven out." These were thoughts habitual to his mind, and his face did not alter as he listened. But when the Superior said, "We have just been to see Canon Le Suet; he told us the Mother-House could not take us in, so that we must go back—go into the world again——"

"Into the world again!" cried the priest. His eyes dilated, in the energy that never ages, shining with a pointed light, the lofty light that saves from shipwreck.

"My poor children, I suffer with you. Your

Community is to die, and your enemies are glad of what your friends, as yet know nothing of. And these perfect souls, these saints—for there are saints amongst you—they were the work of centuries of daily grace. And how long will it be before the slow making of saints can begin and can work on to that end again? It is easy to say 'Go back to the world,' but you have never really lived in it; you are not fit for it; you have not passed through the novitiate of worldly life. You are not called; you are not ready."

They held down their sorrowful heads. "Yes," he said again, "I am much afraid. Delicate flowers are soon faded; there will be some spoilt souls. And amongst those who will remain, how many will abate their early loftiness of life!"

He saw that Danielle was weeping.

"Forgive me, I ought not to make you cry. What I have said will not, I trust, be true of you."

"What are we to do?" said Sister Justine, harping on her one note.

"You have no choice. You will be dispensed from your vows of poverty and obedience. You will have to live in a middle state full of dangers. You, Mother, will you not try to find shelter for as many of your daughters as you can?"

"I have very young ones."

"I know. You must pray once for the old nuns and twice for the young ones. You will pray amongst the perpetual difficulties of the life before you. And that is a prevailing prayer. It should be, if the sum of virtue is not to be lessened in France."

He rose and paced the narrow room, his head bent.

"And take notice, Sister Justine, that though you are no longer Superior, you are none the less responsible."

"Yes, Monsieur l'Abbé."

"Will you promise to forsake none of them?"

"I love them all. But for the present moment, Monsieur l'Abbé?"

"For the present you must go with dignity, as with dignity you will one day die."

"It is like death," whispered Sister Danielle.

"In the first place, you ought to hold your usual prize-giving."

"And say good-bye to our little girls, to their mothers, to the old girls, to everyone? I thought so too. Ah, I am glad you agree."

She had resumed her old expression of burly contentment.

"You are too weak to resist," added the priest, "but at least let right and justice make a good end, knowing that they will rise again. Do not go of your own free will, but submit to force. There need be neither blows nor outcries, but there should be witnesses able to say some day, 'They did not forsake us; they were driven out; they would be glad to come back; let us call them!'" He turned abruptly to the two women. "You are penniless, are you not?"

"No, Monsieur l'Abbé, we have each forty francs which the Canon gave us, from the Community. They can do no more for us."

He paused, as though thinking something that

he did not utter. Then he raised his hand, and the Sisters knelt.

"I bless you," said the priest.

They rose, bowed, and, the one following the other, passed down the steps and out into the street.

Ten minutes later the Abbé Monechal went out in his turn, and taking his shabby hat, shaggy except where the brim was bare—he habitually lifted it to many very insignificant people—he walked towards the Saône. Following the Quai Saint Vincent, at the foot of the Croix Rousse, he passed the narrow gorge of the river with its high banks, and climbed the steep avenue of the Cours des Chartreux.

Almost at the summit, in a plain house, the remains of an ancient palace now half destroyed, had lived M. Talier-Décapy since the now distant day of the death of his wife; and there he lived alone. He had withdrawn from his business some months before; and he was dying. With him a great commercial name, one of the most honourable in the silk-industry, would come to an end. He was a hard-working man, absorbed by affairs from his youth up, slow to form a decision, but tenacious when he had put his hand to any task; he had established either factories or agencies in Persia, in India, in Japan, in the United States; he followed closely the course of commerce throughout the world, was well informed and very sure of himself as to the few questions that greatly interested him, and had trebled the considerable capital of his inheritance. Having lived,

besides, for seventy years on the interest of his
income solely, he had added another fortune to his
capital. He had no taste for expenditure, but he
was not miserly. He had no light sense of the responsibility of riches. And this had urged him to
say to his friend the Abbé Monechal: "If you
should know that my end is near, tell me."

The priest had never doubted his affection nor
his fortitude. But the ascent to the old man's
house was made with pain, and slowly, for the
errand was a hard one. When he rang, it was
done hastily, without a pause for thought. The
footman admitted him without waiting for his
question: "How is he?"

"Very ill, Monsieur l'Abbé. His heart jumps
so. He still walks about, but he sleeps in his
chair."

"And there is not much sleeping to be done
there, I know that," said the priest, who was
obliged to pause at the foot of the stairs, for he
was one of those whom, little by little, grief de-
stroys. On the second floor the footman led him
into a large room lighted by four high windows,
two of which were open to the west and two to
the south.

"Why, it is the Abbé," said a yet unbroken
voice.

A little slender man, wrapped in a dressing
gown, lifted himself, with three careful efforts,
from his armchair by one of the southern windows. M. Talier-Décapy was built for activity,
but something had come to pass to tame his
vivacity of movement.

"Well, Monechal," he said, having recovered his breath, "it is three months since you last came to see me. And I am ill enough!"

"I have so many poor patients, my friend. The rich ones have their comforts."

"But I have none, except perhaps this view of Lyons. That, I confess, is pleasant for a helpless man. Come and see."

He bowed, with a ceremony curiously in contrast with his manner of addressing his friend in the second person singular, and allowed the priest to stand in the full light at the open window. He meanwhile watched the eyes of his visitor as they in turn watched the Saône and the storm-cloud coming across the sky.

The priest's face wore a look that was deliberate and very grave.

"In your eyes," said the sick man, "I can see the whole city."

The other made no motion.

"I see the river in your eyes; it is so bright— I am sure there are barges there, and the Scorpion tugging them towards Vaise. There is the spire of Saint Paul's, the two spires of Saint Nizier, the dome of the Hôtel Dieu, the innumerable roofs of the Terreaux and of Bellecour. But how serious you are, Monechal! What are you looking for?"

"I am trying to count the churches and the Sacred Hosts that are keeping guard over Lyons. Will you kneel with me?"

M. Talier-Décapy knew his friend too well to be surprised; he knelt.

For a minute there was no sound in the room.

The priest rose first, and raised the old man, before whom he stood leaning against the window-post.

"And so," he said, "you are no better?"

"The doctor would like me to think I am better, and so I let him explain to me the many symptoms of my recovery. But all the while I know I am very ill."

"And you are right," said the priest, with meaning.

The other had a sudden giddiness from the shock, and for an instant he closed his eyes as though the light hurt them. He showed that the blow had told, though he did not wince, and hardly grew paler. But his eyes fastened passionately on those of the priest, which did not turn away, did not seek by any softening look to mitigate those significant words, yet were troubled and soon bright with tears. Of the two men the most moved was the priest. "I promised to tell you," he said at last; "I am keeping my promise."

"Everyone else would have deceived me to the end," answered the sick man. "Thank you. And do you know whether it will be long?"

"Do what you would do if it were not for long."

Then followed a passage of silent communication between the two men. The thought of death, like the thought of their friendship, united them, and filled the moments they were living through. In at the window came the sound of the city, and over the horizon a cloud like a sack of grain was letting its rain fall through.

M. Talier-Décapy lifted his bent shoulders and took the hands of the priest.

"What ought I to do, my friend, with the heavy fortune I am to leave behind?" And he added, without sadness: "It was a fortune difficult to get, not easy to keep; I should like to leave it usefully. I shall not disinherit my cousins; I want them to have a reasonable sum. But when one comes to the pass I now am at, one thinks of many things that might be done. Will you help me?"

"No, not I," said the priest decisively. "But if I have any advice to give you it is that you should act according to your feeling for this city of yours. Go through these streets, notice what you see, remember it. And when you have drawn up your list of legatees, I shall ask you to give a thought to one poor woman."

"Who is she?"

"You know that the Sisters of the Place Saint Pontique are to be evicted?"

"I did not know it."

"In a few days."

"Ah, Monechal, I am glad to be leaving this world and to be on my way to a place of justice! And you wish me to make a bequest to one of the Sisters?"

"It would be well—to the Superior; a small sum. They are all poor, and they ought to be poor. Their trial is to be a trial, but it must not be too crushing. Will you go to them?"

"Yes, I promise. And will you see me again?"

The priest could not reply. He rose, and the

two friends took leave of each other gravely, the heart of each filled with an unuttered admiration. Hardly had M. Monechal left him when the manufacturer told his servant to telephone for the carriage. Two hours later, much fatigued, having driven through a great part of the city, and drawn up a long list of legatees, M. Talier-Décapy drove to the door of the school on the Place Saint Pontique. It was with difficulty that he held himself erect.

Sister Justine received him in the little parlour to the right of the front door. She came quickly, with her own serene and active manner. He did not know her; he had expected to see an anxious woman in tears, and involuntarily he showed his surprise.

"Are you not turned out of your convent, Sister?"

"Ah! yes—we are indeed."

"Is it to be soon?"

"At once."

"I should wish to have your address—your address after the eviction. I might have something to say to you, or some little help to give you. I can but suppose that you will need some help?"

"If you could tell me where we shall find a shelter a week hence I should be glad," said Sister Justine, with a laugh. "Not one of us has any idea what is to become of her. Let me have by post what you are pleased to give us—it will be sent after me."

"Unless hands are laid upon the money with

all the rest. My poor Sister, let me tell you that business does not seem to be your strong point."

"Well, hardly. But neither am I good at making excuses for my defects," she replied.

M. Talier-Décapy noted in writing the family name of Sister Justine, and when he was again in his own room he added this to his list: "My heirs will also find out the place of residence of Madame Marie Mathis, in religion Sister Justine, late Superior of the school in the Place Saint Pontique, and will place at her disposal the sum of three thousand francs, to be applied to the benefit of the Sisterhood."

He did not know that he was indirectly giving succour to the little Pascale Mouvand, the child of the master-weaver who had so long worked for him, and who had died at his loom while weaving a court dress for the coronation of the English King.

*   *   *   *   *   *

On the evening of the same day, in the room in which they met when the weather prevented their out-of-door recreation, the five nuns were again together. They had taken chairs, and they sat in a semicircle at the window, in a dusk, that was now and then shattered by lightning. And at every flash the gleam showed one or two of the gentle hands making the sign of the Cross on frontlet and white breast. The Superior was telling the story of the afternoon's two visits. She announced the inevitable end of community life, the necessity for each to go out into a world abjured five years ago, ten years ago, twenty years ago, forty years ago, and to seek a shelter, labour, daily bread. The four were motionless at the close. There were no comments and no questions. The rain rattled sharply as hail upon the window-panes. After a long silence the Superior resumed:

"You will write, dear children, to ask your families to receive you, at any rate until I may have found situations for one or two as school-teachers. No doubt it will take time."

Sister Danielle and Sister Edwige bent their heads in assent.

"I have no family left," said Sister Léonide.

"And I have only a cousin," said Sister Pascale, "and she lives a long way off."

"I wished to speak to you about that matter," said the Superior. "Stay here while the others write their letters."

The Superior and Sister Pascale remained together. The fading day, the coming stars, as the clouds dispersed, showed the white face and white veil of Pascale, her hands folded on her knee, her lips apart, as she caught her breath in distress.

"My little Sister Pascale," said the old nun, "it is for you that I am most anxious. You are so young!" she added in her sad thoughts, "and so lovely. You have distant cousins at Nîmes? Yes, but before I entrust you to them —you, my treasure, the most fragile of my treasures—I must know something of them. Are they really good people; shall you be safe in their house if I let you go?"

"But where else *can* I go, Mother? I have not learnt any business."

She coloured. For when, a few moments ago, she had heard that the breaking up of the community was not to be avoided, she had been aware—even in the keenness of her grief and in the midst of her sorrowful sisters—that the thought of Nîmes was much alive in her mind. She had vividly recalled, in quick mental vision, the house of the Prayous, the hill of Montauri, the neighbouring city, and had remembered the days in which she had received—she, poor Pascale—those unaccustomed attentions, that novelty of homage. Her youth, she felt, was stirred; well versed in the art of self observation, alert in marking the motions of her heart, the young nun knew that a thought of pleasure was within her; she knew that perilous was this pleasure. And she had already yielded to its temptation when she had made her vague and evasive answer.

"You have not learnt a business," Sister Justine proceeded, "and of all my children you are the most delicate and least fitted for work. Your lungs are weak. Until I can place you in a school—if I ever can—a country life in the South would be perfect for you. But tell me, would you be spiritually safe?"

Sister Pascale did not meet the Mother's attentive and anxious eyes. She glanced away at the night sky. She was troubled, because the responsibility for her own future was, by this question, laid upon her acknowledged weakness. She answered:

"I don't think he would be dangerous for me.

He will remember that I am—perhaps he is married by now. As for my aunt, she was really like a mother to me."

The rain fell afresh. There was a sound of running water in the deserted *place*.

"Then you will write to Nîmes," said Sister Justine, and the two women rose.

* * * * * *

On the morrow, which was the 20th of June, and a Friday, the Sisters were definitely informed of the day which was to be their last together, and of the treatment they were to receive. Ursula Magre had sent the required report to the chief of police, who was satisfied that with a little diplomacy he would be spared the unpleasant necessity of violence against women, with the spectacle of shattered doors, of forcible entry into bolted cells, with the noise, the protests, the whole display of house-breaking, which the spectators are apt to take ill. A timely word on behalf of the Mother-House had made all smooth. A *commissaire* called on the Superior. He was a jovial-looking man, who at the first glance seemed more than good-natured—familiar, and on acquaintance proved to be so. He took the tone appropriate to his character, and as he thought, to the occasion. Sister Justine received him, standing in the corridor, a few steps within the door.

"My poor lady," he said, "my business is not always a joke for me——"

"Mine never is to me," interrupted the Superior. "You have come to expel me?"

"No, Madame. Compose yourself, and let us have our talk without losing our tempers. I have called with the order for closing the school and for vacating the premises——"

"Which are our own property."

"That is not my business. They have to be vacated. I am not an unkind man, and I am willing that you should choose your own day, but on condition that there shall be no disturbance, no kind of demonstration whatever. The matter is in your own hands."

"I know it is."

"Then we understand each other?"

Deeply humiliated, her hands idle at her side, very careful of her words, so that she might in no way compromise that dear house at Clermont, in which the race of saintly women might yet be suffered to survive, yet keeping her eyes level and abating none of the dignity of her defeat by any word or tone of entreaty or of fear, Sister Justine informed the police emissary of her resolution. She desired a delay of a week in order to prepare for departure. She desired to hold the prize-giving as usual. She wished that last gathering to be on Friday, the weekly day of the Passion. She asked that a police agent should lay hands upon her shoulders, as on those of an arrested criminal. She would leave on the evening of the same day. On her part she engaged not to spread the tidings of the expulsion, and not to allow the hour of departure to be known to any but the Sisters themselves.

The man made a show of quarrelling with the

terms, but finally agreed. He had obtained precisely what he had been sent to secure.

The week that followed was much like the last week of all other scholastic years. When the mistresses announced to the classes that the prize-giving would take place on the unusual date of the 27th there was much surprise. On the morrow the parents protested. Some of them threatened to take away their girls if the holidays were to be made so intolerably long; a few sus-pected or understood, and the clamour subsided. Within the school the examinations proceeded, the lists were made, and the Sisters were up late at work on the correction of exercises. They tried to talk of the "fête," as they used to do. Sister Pascale and Sister Edwige had orders to make the garlands of green box wherewith the schoolroom had always been hung. Until the last moment, order and tradition governed the life of the convent. A young girl of the district helped them in this last labour—Louise Casale, an ironer, obliged by anæmia to forego the labour and the atmosphere of the ironing-room. She had not been a pupil of the convent, but had been educated at a lay-school in total ignorance of all religion, in spite of which the thing they had not taught her had strongly attracted her heart, so that for many months past she had watched for opportunities of speaking to the Sisters, of offering them such small services as she had to give, and of showing them her ingenu-ous sympathy. When bringing linen to the house she had made acquaintance, one by one, with all the five; and having heard that the prize-giving was near, she asked permission to help in the "decorations."

"I know a garden," she said, with her southern accent, "where there is a great deal of box to spare. The gardener is a friend of mine—only just a friend, mind you. Though I have been brought up in the *laïque*, I am an honest girl all the same."

"You have the eyes of one, Louise," Sister Justine had answered her. "No one will ever make a mistake about that. Shall I show you how I believe in you? I am going to lend you Sister Léonide for half a day."

Louise Casale clapped her hands.

"Just half a day. You will cut the box together, and perhaps you will find another friend of yours who will carry it home."

She had returned to the convent with a barrow full of "green," and now in the largest room—which was a play-room in bad weather and a theatre once a year, when the Shrove Tuesday play was acted by the little girls—three women, standing in drifts and piles of leaves, tied the sprigs in bunches to long ropes for festoons and wreaths. They carried the box about in their gowns held up by the hems. They were Sister Edwige, Sister Pascale, and Louise Casale. This girl, tall, brown, well built and broad of shoulder, lacked nothing for the bloom of beauty except a richer flow of blood, and of this nothing but her work had robbed her. Her thin cheeks, of extreme pallor, and her narrow nose looked too small for her wide white brows and her great eyes, over-long, and dwelling in perpetual shadow.

It was the eve of the exhibition-day. Louise and the Sisters fastened paper roses at intervals on the garlands, from the stock used already in ten successive years. They required a considerable distance in order to be recognised as flowers, even of paper.

"Here are at least twenty metres," said Louise. "Two metres more, and we have done. What time is it?"

"Half past five," said Sister Pascale. "My hands are all green. I am glad we have not to put up the wreaths till the morning." She added in another tone, "It will be pretty, won't it?"

There was no answer. A noise of wheels outside mingled with the rustling of the foliage within. Then Louise spoke to her in a resolute low voice:

"Sister Pascale, please tell me—don't keep me in the dark."

"What am I to tell you?"

"Why, that you are going. You are going, are you not? Something has happened? Am I right? Have I guessed?"

They were close to one another, like two rope-spinners meeting. They had ceased working. Even Sister Edwige caught the words. She did not look round, but her hands too paused. Sister Pascale could not answer. But she looked at the girl whom chance, and something more, had brought to her side in that supreme hour. And hardly had their eyes met when the two young creatures opened their arms and gathered each other heart against heart, weeping. O mournful and hopeless friendship! Strangers a while ago, met from afar, they would have loved one another, but they were to part forever.

"Forgive me, Sister Pascale," said Louise, "I am sorry. I like you so!"

Sister Pascale took from the fold of her dress a few last sprigs of box, but she seemed to see nothing more of her wreath-making; her little fingers mechanically smoothed the leaves as though they had been millinery feathers that she was putting into shape. Her breast heaved, and her head sank. Louise, taller than she, bent close to the black veil and whispered:

"I am not really pious, as you are, but I love coming here. I have thought about ever so many things. And only six months ago I didn't know you; I used to talk against the Sisters—I did. And now when I think of getting married—. Did you ever think about getting married before you were a Sister?"

"Why, yes," said Pascale, "like all girls."

"Well, sometimes I think I should like the kind of marriage that one would never be sorry for afterwards. Sometimes I think I should—not always."

"Ah! that is not an easy matter."

"You don't understand. I mean a marriage like yours, that one would never be sorry for in one's own real soul."

"Oh, my little girl," said Pascale; "what a time to tell me such a thing!"

"Yes," said Louise. "What a time! I ought to have kept my silliness to myself. Well, it's all over. When you are gone I shall go back and be just like all the others."

Sister Edwige had turned. A stout figure, active and short-legged, had entered.

"Come, my children, in two minutes you must wind up. It's recreation time. I am not turning you out, Louise. Why! what is the matter? What is this tragic look about?"

Louise scattered on the floor the box she had carried in her skirt.

"I am going," she said. "Good-bye, Sisters."

"Does she know?" asked Sister Justine; and Sister Edwige answered, "Yes."

The Superior called down the passage, hoping that her voice would overtake the girl:

"Say nothing, Louise, say nothing, for our sakes."

An uncertain answer was sent back, broken by the echoes, and unintelligible.

"Come to recreation, my children," commanded the Superior.

Sister Edwige and Sister Pascale let go the wreath they had fastened off, and said with one voice:

"It is the last recreation."

And seeing that Sister Justine was already on her way to the terrace, they followed her, keeping together, holding each other by the hand—a thing they had never done before—and walked thus to the end of the alley, where the other three awaited them.

Again they were ranged, three on one side, two
on the other, and the two were Edwige and
Pascale. But to-night they did not keep under
the shed; they walked in the court-yard. The
law, the rule of their vocation called and controlled them. As lovers return to the scene of
their loves, and tread again their own vestiges
and walk in the paths of the beloved past, these
women spent the last hours of their liberty in
the place where their children had lived with
them a full and happy life—their children to
whom they had devoted themselves, who had
been the cause and end of their self-sacrifice, as
they were now the innocent cause of their trouble.
After recreation, they knew, there would be prayer
in church, and no silent meeting to follow, for on
this night they must be busy preparing for the
morrow's journey.

The sun, very low, illumined the dust of the
air, and there was not the least particle or atom
that did not carry light in the golden atmosphere.
A summer day like so many of its fellows was coming to an end amid the labour, the sweat, the pain
of the city. Workmen were still at their post,
employers in their offices, at their tables, at their
telephones. And meanwhile, a loss immeasurable
was about to befall them; for five women were
together for the last time amongst them. When
these were dispersed and gone, innumerable lives
would be made poorer, would be altered, would be
lowered. One kind of riches, less honoured than
another in the world, had come to an end. A
grief, pitied by few, had locked in a last clasp of

farewell five human creatures of whom the world was not worthy.

Sister Léonide had let her fire go out, and would never light it again. All alike controlled their grief. Sister Justine, her face drawn, was resolute to keep up the old tone of motherly jollity that had put heart into her nuns and into a thousand women in trouble. Sister Danielle endured her crucifixion, clinging with all her will to her cross of sacrifice, never cruel to her until to-day. Within her heart she repressed a tempest of indignation and revolt. She ordered words of peace to her lips; she set a smile there, like a knot of ribbon on the cross of a sword. Sister Edwige had lost her serenity, and looked much older; in one night her beautiful eyes, her delicate cheeks, had gathered a setting of slight wrinkles. Sister Léonide kept her customary air, cheerful and alert; her nickel watch, like a great onion, had slipped below her waist-belt, and she consulted it as though her office as time-keeper was the chief thing in her mind. Sister Pascale stood in tears, looking at each of her companions. To-morrow Sister Danielle and Sister Edwige would be gone to their relations, far away and far apart. To-morrow Sister Léonide would set off for the village, where, at the last hour, a position as assistant teacher in a free school had been found for her. To-morrow she, the Lyons girl, would have left her city for Nîmes, and the roof of her aunt.

The five women paced the court-yard between one wall and another.

"My children," said Sister Justine, "you must

think, as I do, of the generations of little girls we have known here. We have watched them at play where we are standing."

They trod the dust trampled by those little feet. One cast her eyes upon the sand, with its intricate and innumerable foot-marks; another looked at the schoolroom windows; another followed with her eyes the flight of a flock of sparrows that came to take their customary possession of the place towards night-fall. They thought of the little daughters of working men for whose benefit all had been done—the stones built up into walls, the roof-tiles set, the ground levelled, the cement floor laid, and their own lives spent; half of one life, a little less of another, the greater part of a third. Soft voices, sweet looks, deep-reaching words, dear confidences, faults and falsehoods reproved, ardours and passions that alarmed these watchful mistresses, fervours that delighted them —all, all those childhoods were remembered.

"We must pray for them all every day, every day as long as we live; that will be our perpetual presence in this dear place. Promise!"

Bowed heads replied. Sister Justine held in leash the emotions of these four younger women. Her soldier blood, aware of the moment for command and the moment for relaxation of discipline, told her that there was no danger of coldness or forgetfulness among these daughters of her heart, but that she had now rather to harden them against too painful a tenderness towards their lost children.

"To-morrow, Sister Léonide," she said, "reveillé at five minutes to five. We shall begin the day of trial by hearing Mass. After that you will nail up the wreaths. I want the children to keep a pleasant recollection of their last term. Let them see cheerful things about us, as it will be difficult for us to show them cheerful faces. At ten minutes to nine you will put the parents and the children in their places. You, Sister Pascale, will have charge of the little girls; you, Sister Edwige, of the grown-ups."

"And when do we go?"

"I shall give you the time."

"By what street? Are we to go together? Where are we to turn, Mother?"

The sun went down. Sister Léonide pulled up her watch, anxious that the evening should not overtake her with her task unfinished. They were silent; and a single thought that had not been far from each now took possession of them all. They had not yet suffered the utmost. The moment, the brief moment of real parting had come, for to-morrow no one must weep; to-night they might be weak and weep. The five women stopped in the corner of the court-yard, to the east. They drew together. Hardly, from any window of an overlooking house, could the little group of blue homespun gowns and black veils be perceived in the twilight. And if they were seen, what mattered it? The Superior held out her arms.

"Come," she said, "my children, and let me kiss you. And now if you have any last requests to make, the time is short."

The four nuns, successively in the order of their age, came to her heart and took the kiss of peace. Their Mother having kissed them on either cheek, traced on their brows the sign of the Cross. All her tenderness, human and religious, was in her action. When she took into her arms the youngest of her daughters—Pascale—she held her, unable to let her go, or to say any more than those weeping words:

"O dearest! O dearest!"

Then she turned towards the house, and Sister Léonide followed her; for the last time the night bell was to be rung. The three others lingered. The grave, the wise Danielle took by the arm the youngest of the Sisters.

"I loved you dearly, dearly. I shall love you in my prayers. I should never have told you, if the end of our life together had not come. Good-bye, little Pascale. Keep yourself for God."

She pressed the arm of the young Sister, who was weeping, and who answered in broken phrases:

"And I—I always had a great affection, a great admiration—I shall never hear your name without finding it a support to my weakness. I shall never think of you without feeling a better woman— because of the example——"

But already the slender figure had withdrawn; that soul of sacrifice denied itself a useless emotion; she went away, leaving the young Sister, whom another joined. This was one who was not quite able to restrain her tears, one of less iron courage, one who had never ceased, for two and a half years past, to show Pascale how much she loved her.

"If we are not too poor, and I should ever be able to call you near me, I will send for you," said Sister Edwige.

"You are uneasy about me?"

"Ah, yes, I am uneasy," said Edwige's touching voice.

"Don't be too anxious. I shall be all right— I hope, I hope——"

"Not as you are here."

"But where should I ever be as I am here? I am very unhappy. I had all my peace at Saint Hildegarde's because I always said to myself, 'It is for life!' And now, and now——"

The bell rang, and the two young figures, drooping, passed into the house, apart, speaking no more to one another, their feet effacing the footsteps of their children.

The night came, and she who for five-and-twenty years had directed the Sisters, the classes, the children, the former pupils, and the many clients of the school and the convent, withdrew to her cell—a servant's garret, furnished with a small bed, two chairs, and a black table. At more than sixty years of age she was to leave—no doubt for ever—the scene of her long and willing sacrifice. Before she unpinned her veil, she stood before her plaster crucifix and examined herself.

"Have I allowed the Rule of our Order to grow lax, to grow stale? Have I lessened the time of prayer? Lengthened the time of leisure? Broken without strict necessity the evening and the morning silence? No, I believe in my conscience, I have done none of these things. Have I held the balance of my soul level amongst my Sisters, and amongst my children? My God, I remember the dead I have loved, I know the living I love. And surely I have felt attractions and affections, and particular sympathies. But where this personal love was not, Thou, O Lord, hast put charity into my heart in its place. I think I was not unjust. I have been disgusted by hypocrisies, by dirt, by evil odours, by the insistent claims of poverty; perhaps I have shown my loathing.

"Have I safeguarded the virgins entrusted to my fostering care, and to the shelter of this Order? Well, there is Sister Léonide, who runs about the town at her work. There is Sister Danielle, who has often visited with me the houses of the poor. These two might walk through fire unsinged. The other two have known here nothing of the world except the children, and the wind that blows in at the doors. Their eyes are frank, their gaiety is innocent and young. Even Sister Danielle is a joyous creature, and if she does not speak of her joy, she cherishes it in silence. Even Pascale, who is steadfast only because she is propped and stayed by others, has had a free spirit and a light heart. She has been happy, I think, until these last days. Many of my daughters have kept the absolute sinlessness of their baptism, and carried it to the grave. As for me, I am old, I have never been afraid of plain speaking, and I have had the grace to forget nearly all the evil I have seen, in the hard work of trying to put it right. My

Sisters have had the safety of this enclosure, of perpetual occupation, of their fatigue with tiresome children, of the Rule, of their prayers, of my constant maternal presence; above all, of the continual sense of Thy Presence, my God.

"Have I failed in my duty as a teacher? I have had my pride—my vanity—in the examinations. I have been keen about certificates, and well-written pages, and exercises without a mistake, and correct answers. It is possible that my little girls thought these things more important than they are. There was nothing important but Thou alone. It is of Thee they will have need, in their homes, in their griefs, and in their death. Ah, I fear I did not show plainly that I was first of all a teacher of divine things. My little girls have so much need of Thee. They die so young—often of the second child; and after they have left school they seldom hear a word to lift them up or strengthen their souls. They have so much goodwill, such a secret sense of honour, so much love of God hidden away—it comes out now and then, they remember their home here, and all they were taught that was good; they are loyal at heart. What, what will become of me? If I am to teach, I shall certainly have less human vanity about it. I entreat Thy pardon. It is so difficult not to have preferences for people. I shall try to do better."

She interrupted her simple prayer.

"Twenty-five years," she said. "I thought I should die here. I have examined myself. I have found human weakness, but my God has not been offended. This is only a trial, and I accept it."

At a few minutes before nine, Sister Pascale and Sister Edwige, standing on ladders, hammer in hand, were fastening up the long green wreaths, giving symmetry to arches and festoons, replacing fallen paper roses. The last nail driven in, they came down. Three little girls of some twelve years old—two poor, spare figures and one fat—were sent to open the doors. And at once began the sound of shuffling feet and of voices in every tone of excitement: "Don't push so!" "Take care of your dress—you are tearing it." "Where is the hurry—what are you crowding for?" "What a lot of wreaths! And such nice box— I should never have the patience." "What about the prizes? Are you going to have one? Well, not a very big one?" "Go up, there's your place. Don't you see Sister Pascale? She beckoned to you."

Sister Pascale stood on the right of the platform with the prizes—books, bound in red, blue, and gold—on a table at her side. The older girls were to be on the left. Families and friends sat together, and all talked. Mothers, grandmothers, grown-up sisters, aunts, great-aunts, neighbours, and even—notwithstanding that is was Friday— two or three men filled the seats within a few minutes. The school-children left their family groups, and the sound of kisses was audible among other noises, and wishes of "Good luck!" But among the crowd some were attentive and observant; a rumour had reached them. "They say something has happened. Have you heard anything about the school?" "Why, no." "It would be a pity." "Just look at Sister Pascale's face—there, at the end, where the little ones are sitting." "She got quite red. Who was it spoke to her?" "The little Burel girl—no, Aurelia Dubrugeot, and she brought her a present." "What was it—a cushion?" "No, something that opened; it looks like a valise." "Is it true, Mere Chupin, that the Sisters are going?" "No, my good man; they say so, just to get up a feeling against the Government." "All the same, Sister Pascale looks very unhappy. Poor little Sister Pascale! There's a soft heart for you!" "Look, now she has put the valise in a corner with a cover over it. Aurelia is crying. If you ask me, I don't believe the Sisters are going to be turned out at all. What should they be turned out for?"

The man who had spoken, Goubaud by name, kept a wooden face, with bent brows, and a hand twisting his beard. He looked steadily towards the corner to the right, where Sister Pascale was ranging thirty little heads, dark and fair, and drawing her hands from the clasp of the children trying to kiss them.

"Don't go, don't go away, Sister, little Sister." The golden eyes, the tender eyes of Pascale were wet with tears. It was true that Aurelia had brought a box—a card-board box covered with American cloth, for which her family had no use. Another, a pale child of six, who had one blind, blank eye, and one as blue as heaven, came up with her two hands concealing some-

thing precious. She called louder than the rest,
"Here, Sister Pascale, I brought this for you. I
took it off the mantelpiece." Sister Pascale put
out her hand, and the beaming child laid in it a
pink shell with many spikes. "It's for you,
because I like you." She too knew of the parting
at hand; she too had heard. Others laughed.
Goubaud said to those about him: "We shall
know in a moment. There's the Superior. She,
at any rate, doesn't look unhappy. But she never
does, and looks don't count. She is the stout
one."

"She hasn't got stout by taking care of herself," said his neighbour, who missed his meaning.
"It's not fat, Père Goubaud, it's her age." The
speaker was sixty, but she had "kept her figure,"
inasmuch as she was as flat as a board and
looked like a weasel. "Why, there's none of the
clergy on the platform. That never happened
before."

There was no priest. Sister Justine, with a
mighty effort, mounted that eminence. The
audience coughed, and some chairs scraped.
Sister Danielle, pale, and looking like Justice
appearing among men, entered and sat straight
against the wall; the Superior, much eclipsed
by the tables and the prizes, raised her hand to
speak; Sister Pascale quelled the last two or
three little girls clinging to her skirt; Sister
Edwige, slender, sad, graceful, obviously a lady
in spite of her self-abasements, moved up from
her work of arranging places, took her stand to
the left of the platform, and pulled from her

pocket a paper covered with admirable copper-plate writing—the prize-list, a single copy. Sister Léonide was probably nailing up boxes or closing doors, and was not to be seen.

"I wish to explain to the parents of pupils," said Sister Justine, whose authoritative voice imposed silence, "that it is not by our own wish that we have changed the date of breaking-up. The exhibition to-day will not be as formal as usual. We shall have no singing. We are very sorry to have to send home your children so soon; but we were requested to do so, on account of circumstances——"

There was an interruption. Some irrepressible voices called, "They are evicting you. You may as well tell us."

"Be quiet, Goubaud, can't you?"

"Of course they are not going at all."

"I tell you they are."

"Do listen to the Sister; she can't speak with the noise."

"You *are* an ignorant man, and no mistake!"

Sister Justine imposed silence again.

"No noise!" she cried. "All who are our friends will listen quietly to the reading of the prize-list, and will then go home. As for us, I am glad to think that we have done our best to serve you."

"That you have, Sister."

"Then you are really going?"

"No, can't you understand?"

"Hush! Silence!"

Children were crying aloud.

"Read the prize-list, Sister Edwige," said the Superior.

They were as silent as though called upon to listen to soft music. The music was the voice of Edwige reading out the names. And they were silent also as the prize-winners, by threes and fours, rose and went forward to receive a book, or a green paper wreath, and left little trails of excitement behind them in the crowd.

This lasted until half-past eleven. Then the deafening noise of talk and movement arose again into the atmosphere, now close and heavy with the odours of poverty. The people were going; they had paid their last visit to the school; the district was gathering back its little girls. No doubt these people did not forget the Sisters; but the haste of departure, the crowd, the desire for fresh air, the attraction of the street, the thought of the wine-shop, the mere example of the rest— all these poor trivial motives, with the addition of their shyness and their awkward lack of all in- itiative, left very few indeed to take leave of the school-mistresses where they stood close to the platform, in a little group of the children that were the most affectionate, the vainest of their prizes, or the most forlorn and friendless of the school.

"Good-bye—*au revoir*—Sister Justine, Sister Danielle, Sister Edwige, Sister Pascale."

The nuns bent to kiss the children, pressed the hands of the few mothers, made vague replies to embarrassing questions. And soon they were alone. Mechanically they had retreated to the wall, and it propped their weary figures; they

stood there motionless with idle hands, released
from the necessity of the ceremonial smile, and
watching the backs of fathers, mothers, relatives,
and little girls of all sizes, going away for ever:
their friends going away, the clients of their charity, who had needed them, to whom they had
ministered—their only treasure, their only riches.
They knew many of those backs by the clothes
that the wearers never changed. Each Sister felt
the cruel price at which human gratitude is won;
so much patience, so much self-forgetfulness, so
much persevering effort, in the differing cases of
so many children, to buy a kiss, a softened manner,
a friendly thought, from but one of those who
were going by threes and fours along the school
corridor and out of a door they would never cross
again. There, before their eyes, their work was
falling to pieces.

A slight caress drew Pascale from that sorrowful vision. Close to the platform the young par-
entless child who had one dead eye was still standing. There had been no one to beckon her out,
and she lurked near those who had been kind to
her. Guessing them to be unhappy, seeing them
silent and motionless, she stroked with her little
fingers the hanging hand of Pascale.

"It is Marie," said the young Sister. "If I
could only take her with me!"

The child was clasped in the arms of them all,
and then she went alone, with the noise of her
wooden shoes, looking back at intervals, as though
to say, "I can see you still." The door closed
behind her, and she was the last.

"The time is very near," said Sister Justine.

They listened for the coming of the police. Sister Danielle, deeply troubled, had run to the parlour, to the surprise of her companions, and looking through the window which opened on the *place*, cried to the others:

"There is hardly anyone outside now—they are gone home to dinner."

"The nuns had been at a loss how to pass the last hour or two hours remaining to them, for all their tasks were finished and their duties fulfilled. Danielle's last word reminded them that they had taken nothing but coffee that day.

"We cannot afford to lunch in town," said Sister Justine.

"Have we anything in the house, Sister Léonide? Where are you, Sister?"

The portress appeared.

"We have some bread, Mother, and a half-bottle of wine."

"We will take our last meal here then," said the Superior, and she made once more the gesture habitual to her, half opening her arms to marshal these daughters of hers. Sister Léonide had already left the room, in order to set the table in the little refectory leading out of the long hall, where these poor nuns were accustomed during the winter—and often during the summer as well —to feed children who lived at a distance or were in want. Now, seated about the round table, the Sisters ate their bread and drank a little wine and water. They were more at ease, and were able to speak without allusion to what was about to befall them. All was virtually over for them, since they had suffered the separation from their girls and their girls' mothers. When the meal was finished they sat on, except Sister Léonide, who began to clear the table. At that moment there was the sound of the bell. Sister Justine rose, very pale, and gave the order to the others to follow her. She threaded the corridor, and with a firm hand opened the door of the school and convent.

Two men saluted, the one by lifting his bowler hat with a bow, having an obvious desire to bear himself correctly; the other by a mere nod of a bilious and sinister head. These were the commissary of the police and his clerk. Sister Justine drew back.

"You will allow me to come in?" asked the commissary, upright in his frock-coat. He entered without awaiting her answer, pushing one shoulder forward, on account of the vast amplitude of his bust. He did not wish to come to an explanation at the door, where passers-by might be attracted, for a group or two were gathering. His clerk slipped in behind him.

"You are now in the house belonging to two Sisters of Clermont-Ferrand," said the Superior. "You have come to take their property from them."

"As I told you before, that is not my business."

"In their name, sir, I protest."

"But you will cut your protest short, I hope," said the man, who had done the same work before. Sister Justine silenced him with a gesture.

"I shall not make a speech," she said, "but I shall tell you, and you may repeat it, that you are doing three illegal acts; one, in the destruction of my school, which was a school for the poor; another, in the seizure of our property; and a third in expelling us from the place where we have a right to live. And now you can carry out the eviction."

The commissary expressed annoyance.

"I would rather you did not compel me to make this absurd pretence of violence."

"I would rather you made it. I shall not yield without it."

"As you like."

Sister Justine turned her head.

"Are you there, Sisters? Where is Sister Léonide again?" She called her, and Sister Léonide ran down the corridor, breathless, arranging her veil and her sleeves as she went.

"What were you doing?" asked the Superior.

"Mother, I was sweeping out the classroom."

She took her place by Sister Pascale.

"Do what you have to do," said the Superior to the representative of the law. With a little genuine shyness he laid his hand on the black veil covering the shoulder of Sister Justine, and with that hand upon her she went down the steps, her daughters following.

A group of people, who had suspected or had heard more than the rest, lingered at a distance from the convent door, near the church. They were not more than thirty, parents and children. The presence of the police had also caught the

attention of some few passers-by. When the five
Sisters appeared there was a movement of intense
surprise. No one had quite expected that sight,
or had expected to see it at that moment. A
woman's voice was raised:

"*Vivent les Sœurs!*"

Then every living creature within reach began
to run. Police agents appeared, to right, to left,
at the corners of the streets.

"Take your hand away now," commanded
the Superior.

The commissary obeyed the order, and went
up the steps again. From the threshold he
glanced at the gathering crowd, heard the signal
of a whistle, and cried out:

"No disturbance! I shall arrest the first
person who attempts to make a demonstration.
And you, nuns, out with you!"

He went in, closed the door in which was the
little window wherethrough Sister Léonide was
wont to parley with visitors before admitting
them, and thence he looked on. The five women
in their blue gowns were in the midst of a small
crowd; their hands were sought; they heard
eager voices: "Come to us, come to us!"

Sister Justine made a path with her resolute
hands. "Let us pass, good friends," she said.
A voice cried "*Vive la liberté!*" but found no
echo to the ambiguous words. The police agents
were rough with the women, and rated her who
had acclaimed the Sisters.

"Thank you, Louise Casale, thank you, my
little girl," said the Superior, recognising her.

A few men near a tree were hooting "Down with the priests!" Sister Justine moved on. Close behind her walked Danielle, her eyes on a level with the men's, her hands folded, a storm within. Then came Sister Edwige, blushing very red at the embarrassment of this public appearance; her eyes were down, and she caught her hands shyly away from the kisses and tears of the children. Sister Pascale followed, smiling at friends she spied, excited and a little frightened; and at her side, holding her arm, Sister Léonide, as calm as though she had been about her marketing. The group crossed the *place*, and the police, seeing that something like a crowd was gathering, and that a demonstration threatened in the wide street leading to the station, charged the women and children and scattered them. A brigadier called to Sister Justine: "Divide! Three of you by the Cours Charlemagne. Two this way. You can meet later on." He pushed Pascale and Léonide towards the quay. There were no more attempts at protestation. One or two women and children evaded the bar of the police and caught up the three nuns on the way to Perrache. A few distant voices cheered them; counter cheers replied. Then silence showed that the triumph of "law" was complete. A few of the poorest women were weeping as they went home.

The Community met again half-an-hour later at the door of an old house in the Rue de la Charité.

"Madame Bormenat—which floor?" asked Sister Justine.

Directed to the second storey, the Sisters
awaited there the coming of a maid, who evidently expected them.

"Come in," she said, "poor dear Sisters.
Madame will be here in a moment."

As she spoke, she pushed open a tall oak door
turning on copper hinges, and led into a long
room panelled with oak.   Horse-hair-covered
chairs stood, regularly spaced apart, down both
walls; two high windows, looking into a court-
yard, let in two long lines of light.   It was an
old-fashioned Lyons dining-room.

The five Sisters stood together midway.   They
might have taken the austere-looking place for
a richer kind of convent.   Through the opposite
door now entered an old lady of middle height,
slender, shortsighted, and much resembling the
elder wax heads in a hair-dresser's window; so
smooth were her bands of hair, so regular her
small features, touched with a still lively pink,
and unwrinkled, so equal and steady her smile.

"Good morning, my poor Sisters! You have
come to the wardrobe of secularised nuns? Were
you very roughly treated in your expulsion?"

"No, Madame," replied Sister Justine; "but
all the same, our lives are destroyed. *That* is the
violence we feel."

"A martyrdom, Sisters."

"Yes, indeed, a martyrdom."

"Now, let us see your heights," said Madame
Bormenat without further preparation.   "One
tall"—measuring Sister Danielle with her eye—
"four medium. This is Sister Pascale, is it not?

My poor little Sister, you have a very slight figure,
I should think. I happen to have the mourning
costume of a young girl, a friend of ours." She
played the shopwoman with the ease and quiet of
a lady. Opening two closets in the panels, whence
an odor of naphthaline escaped, she unhooked,
and laid upon the nearer chairs, five skirts, five
bodices, five black mantles, recalling the fashions
of the last three years, more or less; a slight at-
tempt had been made to retouch the sleeves and
collars.

None of the Sisters had as yet begun to disrobe.
They looked at these secular garments and remembered the moving ceremony of their religious
"clothing" on the long-anticipated day when
they had received that pure raiment, every part
of which is a symbol, the sign of a spiritual grace,
and blessed by a separate liturgical prayer. Now
they were to put off the dear and sacred dress.

Sister Justine, with a turn of her eyes, with a
motion of her chin, sent each of the four to her
place, and their pale faces expressed the pain of
this last obedience. They raised their hands to
unpin their veils and frontlets, and to unfasten
the homespun dresses, which fell to their feet.
In the place of four nuns, whose aspect, as they
threaded the streets, had been met with a sign of
respect or a look of hatred, stood four despoiled
women in high-necked chemises and gray woollen
petticoats, with their hair—white, brown, and
golden—cut straight along the back of the neck,
like that of sixteenth-century pages, and hanging
from the head—old or young—somewhat in the

shape of a bell. The maid, who had done the same office before more than once, went from one to the other, measuring a skirt, trying on a bodice, putting in a stitch, opening a seam, moving a hook, and in a quarter of an hour the lamentable transformation was complete. By means of hairpins and black ribbon, the unmanageable short hair had been put up, and had been hidden under shabby mourning or half-mourning hats. Sister Justine, her shoulders covered, in spite of the season, with a cloak, stood looking at her four daughters as they came one by one before the long mirror: Sister Danielle, in her distress like a newly made widow; Sister Edwige very shy and deeply humiliated; Sister Léonide saying, "I look like a second-hand clothes dealer. I am certainly pretty ugly, but then I've not seen myself in a glass for a very long time—perhaps that's why I notice it so." And even there she laughed.

Sister Pascale allowed the maid to fasten her hair, while Madame Bormenat with her own hands tried to tie up the thin white locks of the Superior, who, inattentive to her own case, silent and full of thoughts she could not express, fixed her sad eyes upon the mutilated but still lovely hair of the child of Adolphe Mouvand. Did she foresee how it would look anon, when it would be grown again, when its exquisite straw-colour would be gilded by the sun in a ruffling wind? Did she even now admire, with a pang, in a lady's street costume this child of her heart? Sister Pascale returned her look with an affectionate smile that seemed to say: "What a figure they are making of your little girl! I don't look as miserable as Sister Danielle, but I am the most unhappy of all at heart; I am the feeble one, and you all propped me up." Had Sister Justine lost heart, that she was unable to bear the sting of that poor smile? She sprang from the hands that were busy at her gray head, and, with one thin wisp of hair tied by black string on the top and another fallen on her car, she went, her face drawn by grief, to the young girl.

"My little Sister," she said, "wear that quiet black dress as long as you possibly can." Doubtless her painful thoughts continued, for she added: "Why did I ever consent to be parted from you? . . . But come, my child, put on your hat. We are the last."

There remained a black straw hat, decorated with a little wreath of muslin daisies that were crumpled and bent upon their stalks, and a black tulle bonnet composed of ruches, flattened and rusty.

"Here, Sister Pascale," said the Superior, "the bonnet is for you." Sister Pascale at once took up the dingy mass.

"Why, Madame," said Madame Bormenat, "you are not going to wear a hat with flowers? It would be ridiculous!"

"Less ridiculous than you think," said Sister Justine, putting resolutely on her bare white head the little round hat with the drooping daisies. She would assuredly be an absurd figure in the street; what cared she? She had her usual simple and easy manner, her usual unembarrassed tone, as she returned her own thanks and those of her community to the lady presiding over the "wardrobe of laicised nuns"—an acknowledged private charitable institution. The aged lady bowed in reply with a reserved, compassionate smile, and watched the five women—the five de-poetised women—as they went down the stair. They went, no longer guarded, no longer defended against the world, by the veil, the hair-concealing linen, the rosary, signs in all men's sight of their consecration. Two of them carried, rolled up in bundles, their religious dress—Sister Léonide and Sister Danielle. The others were too uncertain of their journeys so to burden themselves; they left their religious habit with Madame Bormenat.

They left the house, they spoke to each other no more. They asked at the station for the third-class waiting room. A corner there was vacant, and they found places on two benches, sitting as much together as they could. The Superior had Sister Pascale on one hand and Sister Léonide on the other. The two others faced them —the two unequal groups of so many past evenings in the playground.

"My dearest ones," said the Superior, "let us end with what will be all our strength when we are apart. We will say the rosary, and our prayer shall not cease until I am alone."

They sought their beads in the pockets of their lay dresses. The murmur of the *Pater*, the *Ave*, and the *Gloria* was hardly audible in the station sounds—the whistle of an engine, the roll of a train, the opening of doors, and the hurrying feet of travellers. No one noticed the women, ill and awkwardly dressed in mourning, leaning together as though one of them were busily telling the story of a recent death. It was so in truth. *Benedicta tu in mulieribus*—it was Sister Danielle who said the first part of the prayers, and the others made the responses. Now and then one of them hid her tears with her hand and fell out of the ranks of prayer, to join again in a little while.

At intervals a porter came to the door to call the names of the stations for which a train was about to leave. The Sisters trembled, but it was not yet their hour. The names of Macon, Marseilles, Ambérieu, were for them the fatal names, and they had not been spoken. There was a little time yet. The man was somewhat like the messenger of execution to prisoners under the Terror. He went back to the platform, and the prayers were resumed. Sister Pascale led the second rosary, and her frail voice had so weary and so tragic a tone that the others all inwardly offered their prayers for that dear one. *Ora pro nobis peccatoribus nunc et in hora mortis nostrae.* Thus in the noisy and dusty waiting-room the Sisters of Saint Hildegarde prayed their last prayer together on earth. . . . A porter cried, "Train for Macon." And two of the five stood up, Sister Danielle and Sister Edwige. For a moment they hesitated—should that prayer break off so that their farewells might be spoken? Not so; Sister Justine took up the response with authoritative emphasis: *Sancta Maria, Mater Dei*—and they

understood that this was to be the one word
worthy of such a parting.

The two who were going bowed to the three
who remained. Sister Pascale closed her eyes,
the eyes that were to look no more on those two
pale faces. A few minutes, and in the midst of
another prayer, she too rose, bowed, and went
out in tears. Two voices behind her faltered but
did not stop. Anon came the train for Geneva,
and Sister Léonide went out alone. The Superior
was left; she ended the *Ave*, and then sat silent
while her companions journeyed away into the
unknown.

IV.

---   .

THE BEARERS OF PASCALE'S BURDEN: JUSTINE.

A keen autumn wind was blowing across the glacis of fortifications, the chilly fields, a provincial town with its factories piled close to the forts, its noisy streets. Evening was closing round, and it was already dark within doors. A few minutes earlier a sunset light had illumined the lion, cut in the rock, of the citadel of Belfort.

In the servants' quarters of a large, unpretentious house that had no garden, but was amply and solidly built, and was the dwelling of the General Commandant, an old butler prepared the silver for the dinner-table. Over his black clothes he had knotted an apron, and as he turned a severe eye upon the rows of spoons and forks, a little footman with a yellow, shaven head attended him with respect and fear. At another side table, an irreverent orderly, in shirt sleeves and yellow waistcoat, proud of his waist and his fair moustache, was arranging the dessert.

"Five and twenty," said the old man to the apprentice footman—"a large dinner-party. The Baron is entertaining the superior officers. You are not to take your gloves off once."

"No, Monsieur Francis."

"You are not to hand the dishes, of course—not for a long time to come. You'll only have to take away the plates. But you can watch me as a lesson."

"Yes, Monsieur Francis."

"He's pretty strict, you know—the Baron."

"Strict!" cried the orderly with a laugh. "Strict! Why, he's afraid of everybody. He's afraid of *us*."

"He's not afraid of me," said the butler quietly. "Let me go on telling the boy what he has to do. You haven't to answer for him, and I have."

The door of the entrance-hall was opened. The orderly looked over his shoulder. "There's that German woman. I say, don't leave that door open—I am catching cold."

The woman did not heed him. She was unfastening the woollen wrap that had been tied over her black bonnet and her face reddened by the cold. Behind her a young man, painfully thin and pale, whose nervous suffering was shown in the spasms of his delicate features, answered the orderly angrily:

"Hold your tongue, Moriot. She is ten times more French than you are. Never—these are my orders—never again dare to insult this lady, or I shall tell the Commandant."

The soldier had turned back to his work, and was patting into shape the mossy lining of a dessert dish. He said no more, but expressed his small alarm at this threat by a movement of his eyebrows and of his smart moustache. The

young man, seized by what it had been agreed
to call a fit of asthma, had thrown himself upon
the woman's arm, clinging to it with violence;
after three or four dry little coughs, he passed
a few haggard moments in the grasp of terror;
evil, horrible evil, was upon him, his open mouth
drew in no air, his lungs were vacant, close to
his beating heart. The old woman, accustomed
to the care of his disease, held up his head tenderly with her two hands. "Come, my little
Guy, it's nothing. You will be all right in a minute." The fit passed off: a little air went whistling
into the boy's chest, terror left the eyes, the mouth
closed and smiled a little. "I'm better," he said.
"It's gone. But wait——."

The door into the billiard-room opened at that
moment, and, framed against the lights within,
appeared the elegant figure of a woman still
young in shape and in movement.

"Is that you, Madame Justine? Is that you,
Guy? I was getting anxious. How is it you are
so late?" asked Madame de Roinnet. She would
not confess a fear that was not of the late hour
only. But she had heard the cough. "Where
did you walk?"

"On the glacis of the Barres fort, as we generally do," answered the old woman. "It was
almost warm, the sun was out, but all of a sudden
the wind got up, and we made haste home. Perhaps we walked a little too fast."

Madame de Roinnet paid small attention.
Question, answer, the whole situation, were but
a part of that tragedy of her maternity which

she and all about her were resolved to ignore.
She saw her son standing in the middle of the room
between his companion, "Madame Justine," and
the butler; she saw that he had his breath again,
but she heard how hard he drew it still.

"You had better go to your room, Guy, and
get warm. Go, my dear. Madame Justine, will
you come this way? I want to speak to you."

The two women went into the billiard-room,
the one in evening dress, the other in a plain
black gown, worn without any affectation of
singularity—such a dress as is usual with elderly
ladies whose appearance is neither fashionable
nor conspicuously unfashionable.

"Madame Justine," said Madame de Roinnet,
holding on one side her pretty head with its
fair hair turning grey and delicately waved, its
still firm cheeks and youthful blue eyes; "Madame Justine, I have not had a place laid for
Guy at table to-night." She meant "Nor for
you either." Justine understood, and answered
a little sadly: "The poor boy will be rather disappointed. He said just now that he was looking
forward— as for me, you know, Madame, I
don't care a bit. I am even better pleased.
Where are we to dine?"

"Of course not in the servants' hall; shall it
be in the linen room? Only there is a difficulty
about the waiting. Francis cannot leave the
dining-room, nor can the orderly very well; and
Matilda——"

"Oh, is that all, Madame? There is no one
to wait upon us?"

"Well—no, I am afraid not."

"I can very well wait on Monsieur Guy and myself. In our convent we were quite used—I dined every day at the same table as our cook. It was Sister Léonide——"

Madame de Roinnet went towards a group of candles in a sconce, and held her face turned away, as close to the lights as though she sought to dry with that flame the tears hanging on her eyelashes which she would not wipe away. She went on with her inspection, taking her train in one hand, drawing up her graceful figure. "I am obliged to you," she said, "for helping me as you always do. Life is sometimes so difficult." She went her way into the dining-room.

At the same hour at the Military Club, an officer of nervous physique, with signs of race in face and figure, erect in his uniform, thin-faced, grey-eyed, with hair tufted on his temples, his profile resembling some relief of a mediæval Italian warrior traced upon the pommel of a sabre, rose from his place, where he had sat looking through the evening papers, and approached a table where another officer was seated, and, saluting, addressed him. The man to whom he spoke went on with his occupation, which was the sinking of a slice of lemon in his glass of punch. He, too, was tall, with more solid features and with darker eyes, which added emphasis to his words: a man of firmer and steadier type than the other.

"I shall be happy to be with you shortly," he said. "Madame la Baronne de Roinnet is well, I hope? I caught a glimpse of her this afternoon. And your son, how is he?"

The Commandant made an evasive gesture:

"Oh, as for him——"

"By the by, I wanted to ask you: have you still in your house that person——"

"The governess, Colonel? The companion and attendant on my son? You mean, do you not, Madame Justine?"

"Exactly. I am told that Madame Justine comes from a convent?"

With a little shake of body and head, the movement of a man whom the foil has touched at fencing, the Commandant replied:

"Yes, sir, she does."

"She was the Superior of a Sisterhood?"

"She has since been laicised."

"Obviously; and she teaches your children?"

"No, sir; I have had the honour of explaining to you that she walks out with my son Guy, whose health is very far from satisfactory. Madame de Roinnet sometimes sends the little girl out with her too."

"And she gives the children instruction on those occasions most probably?"

The Commandant coloured. All the muscles of his thin face grew tense, and revealed yet more sharply the nervousness of his race.

"If I thought that, sir——"

He faltered; he felt that he was on the point of disavowing his wife, his own hidden religious faith, the principles of his whole life, and the traditions of his family. All the de Roinnets

of the past were at his ear: "Stop! what were
you about to say?"

"If I thought that, sir," he resumed, evading,
"I should tell you so."

"That is well. I spoke in your own interests.
You are ambitious, and quite right too. It is
only fair to warn you of what might be to your
disadvantage."

The two officers parted with a salute. Ten
minutes later M. de Roinnet reached his house
and met his wife in the corridor.

"Marie," he said, "I should like to speak to
you."

"What is it? I am rather in a hurry."

"I hope you are not giving Madame Justine
a place at the dinner to-night. We must not forget that, after all, there are certain differences of
position, of breeding, of manners——."

He lunched and dined daily at the same table
as the former Superior of the convent and school
of Saint Pontique. Madame de Roinnet said
nothing as he pursued:

"If you included her in this dinner party, the
discomfort would be for her, and the embarrassment, as well as for——"

His wife answered with a vague and judicious
smile; "I thought Guy was hardly strong enough
to-night, and he is not dining with us; so Madame
Justine is keeping him company. It is all settled."

That Madame Justine was only barely tolerated
in this household was very evident to herself.
The fact had been made clear to her from the first
day of her arrival, in the preceding August, by the

daily acts, words, or silences of all about her.
After three weeks spent in Lyons in a vain search
for employment, she had had the brief hope of an
appointment to a school which the Catholics of
that city were labouring to establish upon the
ruins of the schools destroyed by law; she had been
judged too old for the position. Such appointments were, of course, much less numerous than
the members of Religious Orders expelled from
their convents or dispossessed of their schools, and
in either case in search of the means of livelihood.
Of the five women who had dwelt together, fully
employed, in the house of the Place Saint Pontique,
only one had found work as a teacher. This was
the portress, Sister Léonide. Then the Superior,
having spent the forty francs which formed her
whole fortune as an ex-nun, had accepted a place
as "governess and companion" in the household
of Madame de Roinnet. She was rather a nurse
than a companion.

Her business—and she did not consider it in
any degree beneath her dignity—was chiefly to
walk out, whenever the weather permitted, with
the son of the house, the poor boy incurably consumptive, and ill in mind as well as in body, who
needed frequent comforting and close nursing.
She had to amuse him, with as little conversation
as possible, to choose pleasant walks, to find
sheltered seats, to avoid acquaintances, for talking
brought on his shattering cough, to take charge
of the plaid and goloshes, to betray no anxiety of
her own, to make no manifestation of her pity
when the attacks of his disease were violent, to

put aside all fears of contagion for herself, to make the dying boy look forward to next spring, next summer, other summers and springs; it was a mission for a mother rather than for an alien. Madame de Roinnet had attempted it, but her tenderness was too demonstrative; she found it too difficult to master her grief, to keep back her tears. Moreover, the work prevented all her social obligations, and she had duties to the Commandant, to his career, and to her little girl, who, the doctors warned her, must not be much in the company of her brother. After she had relinquished the task, ten servants in succession had failed in it, for night-nursing and watching were necessary, as well as perpetual attention by day, and Madame Justine had been called in.

She endured fatigue; she had the necessary patience and also the habit of authority equally indispensable; she succeeded in gaining the affection of the young man who was little more than a gloomy and embittered child, nay, succeeded only too well, for she became the one support, the one resource, and the invalid was excited and angry if ever his nurse was not at hand, not ready in case of an attack, and he—as he said cruelly enough—"all alone." But the cook and the maids lost no opportunity of making Madame Justine feel herself isolated in the house—she, a woman already old and yet dependent, of most distinguished character, of ordinary education, a member of the lower class by early association, by no means a lady, yet in the habit of addressing simply as "Monsieur" the

master they had to call "Monsieur le Baron."
She was an Alsatian, besides, and the orderly—
a doubtful soldier and more doubtful servant,
who disliked the clear-seeing eye of the old Superior
—spread the rumour, readily believed in barracks,
that the Commandant employed a German spy
as governess for his children. Madame de Roinnet
took her part, having opposed the dismissal of the
"companion," several times threatened when the
drawing-room talk in the garrison ran to this
effect: "You know that Madame Justine they
have at the Commandant's? Well, my dear, she
is an ex-nun—a secularised Sister. She was
actually the Superior in a convent!" But Guy's
mother had almost too hard a task in the refuta-
tion of so many unkind suspicions, so many cruel
whispers. She was too unhappy a woman, con-
vinced as she was at heart of the hopeless state
of her son, and involved in troubles of money, to
possess energy enough for the protection of
Madame Justine against those who would have
had her expelled. The nurse's real champion was
her nursling. Almost every day the more violent
attacks of his disease were upon him; he struggled
out of his chair, stifled, his face full of the terror of
the loss of breath, his thin arms outstretched, his
hands clutching. The father turned aside, unable
to endure the sight, or hurried away, or cried to
the unfortunate boy, in the nervous anger of
despair: "What, again? Stop, stop, stop in-
stantly. Stop, I tell you, or leave the room!"
The mother ran to the rescue. But it was on
Madame Justine's breast that the boy cast himself

until the racking cough was over, and on her shoulder that his head rested, bathed in the sweat of the struggle. As the weeks went by M. de Roinnet saw how little hope there was that another would fill her place, or that Guy could bear the separation. And this, too, irritated him; his ambition of standing well with his superiors was hampered by this domestic difficulty.

Madame Justine would have lived, with as much ease as she asked of fortune, in the midst of these small enmities, had she been free from graver anxieties. In her few and uncertain moments of leisure she wrote to "her daughters," and many times every day her thoughts visited those corners of France where, far apart from one another, lived the four whom she so grievously missed.

It was for the youngest only that she was anxious. To the letters in August and September Pascale had answered briefly that she had been kindly received at Nîmes; they treated her with an affection that was touching and even embarrassing, inasmuch as they allowed her to do very little of the work of the house; they considered her health to be delicate, and Jules Prayou took her out a great deal and had tried to persuade her to go to the sham bull-fights and even to the theatre. She held back, not wishing to be an expensive guest with relatives who were poorer than she had thought them, and who were yet generous to her. "Just think, Mother," she wrote, "at Beaucaire, where they have a fair on the 22nd of July, Jules spent for me more than thirty francs, what with the journey, and treats and presents! And you know I have not a penny of my own. I could not stop him. And then afterwards he did the same at Arles. Nobody knows that I was ever in a convent. People think I am here for my health; and, in fact, I am taking care of myself. The heat and the restful life have done wonders for my lungs. I am quite brown, but my hair, which is growing fast, is as light as ever. People stare at me because of my hair. Things come into my mind—things I never thought of in the convent, where we five did not own a looking-glass amongst us. Mother, it is not my chest that troubles me most, it is the heart inside, now you are not there to take care of it."

Sister Justine wrote recommending more prudence and a closer watchfulness. Her letters to Pascale were increasingly affectionate. But no letter from Nîmes had come since the end of September. It was now the 15th of October. Danielle and Edwige wrote: "Neither has she answered our last letters."

What was befalling that distant one? O agonising question! Madame Justine carried it with her in the long hours on duty with her invalid. Her mind was full of misgivings, full of plans. She had no more rest from her anxieties now than she had formerly from the little school-children or the poor of Lyons. At times, as she looked across the bare land to the far horizon and the distant frontier, the thought of her own native country recurred to her: "Within reach of this place there are relatives of mine living.

They would take me in if I wished it; they have
written to tell me so. There is my sister, married
to a vine-cultivator who owns a very good vine-
yard, near Saint Léonard. There is my brother,
who has land of his own at the gates of Colmar,
where I was born. I might go back; the Kreis-
director would give me the necessary authorisation for the asking. I should have nothing to do
but to grow old there and die in peace."

But the thought was against her desire, against
her heart. What she listened to was the voice
within: "I shall go through the trial and trouble
of France. I belong to France, and in France my
four daughters are scattered."

LÉONIDE.

Winter was over for dwellers in the plains, and
the wheat, sprouting green, was tempting the
mating partridges to nest-building. But snow
was on the hills, yielding a little each afternoon
on the heights of Bugey, where dwelt the former
portress of Saint Pontique; each night the frost
returned and stiffened again the old snow, now
trampled and full of holes. The village was built
on a steep south-western slope below a fir-forest
which the peasants pillaged, and the lightning had
seared, and the torrents shattered. Where there
was not forest, there were rocky fields, ravines,
land partly washed away by water, and houses
sheltering where they found a footing. Far below,
in the valley, were meadows set with hedges, almost as regular as dominoes. And so far was it
from the high village to those cultivated lands,

that the cries of the men below goading their oxen
at the plough troubled the silence on the heights
less than did the whirr of the grasshopper.

Here, in a free school newly built, Léonide had
held an appointment as assistant since the July
preceding. A rich woman, who had given the
land for the school and who bore one half of its
charges—the inhabitants of the mountain-side
supplying the rest—had summoned the portress-
cook from Lyons. After a short interview the
patroness concluded:

"Well, my little Sister, I think you will suit
me."

"I am glad of that, Madame."

"Then I shall decide to engage you. I like you."

"Ah! if you had seen Sister Pascale—you
would have engaged *her!* Or else Sister Edwige,
or——"

"But I have engaged *you*, you know, and I
think I shall not regret it. By the way, you will
have a room to the north, I must tell you."

"It is all the same to me."

"And the people here are not precisely religious."

"I can't say they were exactly that at Lyons,
either."

"I only see one little fault in you, Sister."

"You might see plenty if you looked, Madame."

"Well, but I mean that you have lost your teeth.
It does not look well——"

Léonide laughed with all her heart.

"I shall buy some then, Madame. In a fortnight I shall have the whole set."

She went to a dentist before leaving Bourgen-Bresse, and arrived at her new home hardly prettier but much younger of aspect than she had been.

"You would not know me again," she wrote to her Superior, "if you were to meet me on these steep roads, with my handsome new skirt and my hat, and all my teeth; you would only know who it was when I ran to hug you, Mother."

The ardent little school-mistress had no longer the luck of Lyons and Saint Pontique. She ran about, she taught, she talked, she catechised, but without the old cheering success. All the summer, all the autumn, all the winter, in dust, mud, and long-lasting snow, she trudged through all her free hours and her holidays, from house to house of parents and guardians. Many of the guardians were hostile, few of the parents had the ordinary good humour of the city or the valleys. This hard-living mountain-population was full of discontent, was suspicious even in the presence of self-devotion—in which it hardly believed—was unresponsive, quick-witted in buying and selling, armed against things invisible. The better part of these people was no more than a kind of half-aroused indifference and the remains of a faith ancient and remote. "How they must have been neglected!" thought Léonide. "On their very death-beds they hardly remember to look upwards. They are not always kind to me. But they shall not resist me for ever; I shall use the strongest means I know—I will love them, I do love them."

She had walked so much, on paths so steep, and through snow so persistent, that at the be-

ginning of March she had fallen seriously ill with
double pneumonia. But her robust constitution
had won the battle with disease; and, very pale,
very thin, she sat in a wicker arm-chair, covered
with black woollen wraps, her feet on a hot-water
bottle, in the large first-floor room above the classroom of the school. The children had left.
Evening had turned the long white walls ash-grey,
the red cotton bed-curtains made a dark spot in
the pale room. The clanking of wooden shoes
outside was audible, and within, the loud ticking
of the alarum clock. A woman came up the stairs
and entered.

"How are you this evening, Léonide?" she asked.

From the midst of the shawls the invalid answered: "Better and better."

Her voice was weak, but her eyes were bright
in the twilight. With the lively gratitude of the
solitary sick for a visit from outside, Léonide
looked up at the head mistress, a slender young
woman with a long face, a pretty complexion, and
short-sighted eyes narrowed by the perpetual
effort of "accommodation." She kept her chilly
hands in her apron pockets and sat down on the
other side of the fireplace.

"The little girls were asking about you again,"
she said. "You see, they don't forget you. What
I came about was to ask whether you don't want
to go to bed again. I'll help you."

"Thank you; but let me sit up in the dark,
just another hour."

"It's exceedingly cold outside."

"But I'm really coming to life again in here,"

said Léonide, freeing her chin. "Do you know what I was thinking about? First of all I thought how very near I was to going home——"

Seeing the astonishment of her companion, she smiled slowly and pointed her fingers upwards.

"I mean my home aloft," she said. "But it's put off. Then I was thinking of the kind of life I led for ten years with my Sisters. Does it bore you to hear me talk about it?"

"Why, no, of course not," said the young woman rather languidly. She held her long thin hands towards the fire with a patience already half wearied.

"I can tell you I didn't waste my time in those days. You say I wear myself out here; but there I was always on my feet: sweeping, cleaning, cooking, answering the door, washing—I had a lot of work. I was a kind of convent general-servant; and yet, mind you, the others always treated me as their sister—one of themselves."

"Yes, I understand."

"It's a better kind of friendship than any friendship out in the world."

"Well, it's different, anyway."

"That it is."

"Sadder, I should think."

"Sadder, do you say? You should have seen the good spirits we were in. I'm still like that. Sadder—Sister Justine, Sister Edwige, Sister Pascale! Do you mean what you say?"

"Well, I do. I can't understand being happy shut up in a house and having to stay there."

A whole-hearted laugh, a peasant's laugh without the noise of health, astonished the head-mistress.

"Are you happy, Mademoiselle?" asked Léonide.

"Why, yes—fairly."

"Yet you can't go out of the village because of the snow. You have to stay in to teach your class and to take care of me."

There was a silence between those two separated women. Then the mistress rose, put her hands into her pockets again, and said:

"I am going to cook our dinner. In half an hour I shall come back and help you into bed."

Léonide remained alone. In spite of her wrappings she felt the frost that was seizing the earth, the trees, the walls and roof. She leant her head and her shoulders against the back of her chair, and, with the precise perception of one half-released from the world, she measured the greatness of her solitude. At the beginning of her work in that place, when her hard walks to the outlying hamlets and farms had been over, she had slept soundly at night, overcome with fatigue, with no thought of to-morrow except that of the duty to be done. But in this sad hour she judged her efforts to be, at least for the time, in vain. Was there any good will towards her and her mission in all these houses closed against the cold of that bleak country? Was there anyone who really knew, or cared to know, why she had come thither, why she was staying, why she would never wish to change, to "better herself," to marry, or even to complain? No, not even the good girl who directed the school, and who was hoping to make a little money and to get away—to escape, by marriage or promotion, the hardship of this

confinement on a mountain height. All doors, all
hearts, were closed. The alarum was ticking the
flight of futile and vacant minutes. Through the
window the sick woman saw the tops of the dark
and serried fir-woods, her eyes receiving their
image though her thoughts did not dwell upon
them. The ragged mists rolled over those dreary
heights. Untroubled in her grief, trying to smile
again her patient smile, Léonide whispered:

"I accept my failures, my loneliness, my illness,
all things, O Lord, for the sake of my Sisters, but
particularly for the little one."

She had heard vaguely that Sister Justine was
not easy about Pascale. They had told her no
more—why should they? She had never made
a part of the "Council" of the Community. But
in Madame Justine's brief letters she had guessed
a burden of sadness. And thus, in her desolate
and disheartened and disenchanted hour, she
consciously took the trial home to her faithful and
fervent heart: "I accept my poor failures, as
Thou wilt, O Lord, for my Sisters, and particularly
for the little girl."

The formidable night enwrapped the mountain,
the forest, the hill-village; and in a little house
that one fir-tree might have covered with its
shadow, a poor creature was in treaty with the
Eternal for the safety of a soul in distress.

EDWIGE.

Early summer, the warm season when all green
things are not yet out, when the young leaves
seem verily to give out light—the luminous sum-

mer of the end of May—was sweet upon the waters
of the Loire. By the riverside, in the valley,
stood the narrow house of the keeper of a level-
crossing. It was built at a few yards' distance
from the line of the Paris and Nantes railway,
close to a road which came from the hills on the
north, crossed the valley, the fields, and the rail,
and further on passed over the Loire by an arched
bridge. Peasants' carts, traders' carriages, mo-
tors on their way to the country-houses of the
south, came to the crossing at any hour of the day
or night. The guard had to close and open the
gates, and to stand outside the door when the
trains went by. The task was not exacting or
fatiguing, but it needed punctuality and the habit
of light sleep. It needed also no little courage,
for the house of the level-crossing-guard was far
from all other habitation; few were the farms in
these low valleys on account of the frequent
floods.

It was three o'clock in the afternoon. An old
woman, meanly dressed, but with her hair care-
fully arranged in wavy bands, was crouching
over a garden-bed near the house, by the railway
side. She was pulling up weeds from the sandy
ground. Her movements were exceedingly slow,
yet they seemed too much for her strength; for,
at every quarter of a yard of weeding, she stopped
and rested, with her eyes upon the four lines of
flying steel that went converging to the far horizon, where they seemed to meet like the fastened
threads of a loom. The fields on either side of the
railway had their young crops stirred in the light

by the gentle wind. Between rows of poplars
there were gleams in the distance: a little water
and a little sand, like silver and gold.

The woman resumed her work, broke off
again, and watched the line. At half-past three
she called:

"Here comes 717."

No one replied for a few moments, and she
was crouching at her task again when a much
younger woman opened the door and appeared
upright at the threshold.

It was Edwige, lovelier than in the days of
the school at Saint Pontique, inasmuch as her
chestnut hair was visible and her beautiful eyes
reflected a wider sky. But now her look of
heavenly mercifulness rested only on one heed-
less old woman, on the garden, and the fields.
She wore a light bodice and a dark skirt, as do
so many country women, and, by way of protection against the sun, a white cambric summer hat
of English fashion, a relic of better days in her
father's house. When the goods-train reached
the crossing, she unrolled and lifted the red
flag in her hand. For two minutes the earth
shook, the willows had their foliage stirred, birds
went up, the lowing of cattle and sounds of invisible life in the fields arose amid the rattle of
iron wheels; and, as the last truck passed by, a
little shower of sand fell on the vegetables and the
five gooseberry bushes of the roadside garden.

The old woman with the waved hair had not
looked round. Edwige stood for a moment
turned to the distant East with its gleam of

waters. In her face and in all her aspect was
legible the characteristic message of her love.
She went back into the little house, and, as
silence again settled on the place, drew up to the
table again the chair from which she had lately
risen, and took her knitting. At her elbow a book
of Hours lay open; now and again Edwige read
a passage, and meditated upon it as her fingers
moved.

Here she dwelt, and the woman was her mother.
When a station-master of the railway company
in question leaves a widow, as in this case, she
has a right to the holding of a station book-stall,
if such a place be vacant. The mother of Edwige,
a contentious and irritable woman, was insistent
in her claim, but there were several senior widows,
and there was no vacancy. After a time of great
poverty, at first alone and then with her daughter,
in a village of the Blaisois, she had accepted the
post of barrier-guard. She would not have been
unhappy had the thought of a "fall in life" not
harassed her.

On account of her rheumatism she left the
level-crossing and the signal to her daughter,
whom, however, she helped by her keen ear and
her little sleep. By night and day she watched
the clock and cried "Time!" when a train was due
and the road-gates were open, or "Someone at the
crossing!" when the gates were closed.

Edwige felt herself under an obligation to
remain with a mother whose livelihood depended
upon her. She accepted the duty with her whole
will in the spirit of self-sacrifice so familiar to her

thoughts and practice, but never proclaimed.
She too was a widow, but one who held her peace.
She was never found in tears. Her peculiar
tenderness seemed to brood upon the present
passing day. But the day brought two distresses
to be added to her profound and perpetual sorrow. One was in the morning, and one in the
afternoon. Her heart was torn; her mother never
knew it.

The late hour was drawing near. Several times
Edwige had looked at the clock: four o'clock,
five minutes past, ten minutes. And after each
questioning glance her eyes had turned to the
grass-bordered road on her right. Another minute or two and her mother's voice called: "Edwige! quick—there they are! and the express is
in sight!" She ran to the gates, her tender face
pale and drawn. Thirty children, boys and girls,
going home from school, were at the level-crossing,
crying, "Mademoiselle! Quick, Mademoiselle!"
The boys lifted their caps to her, the girls held up
their hands with the fingers out as in class. It
was a clamour of fresh voices and a flash of bright
eyes.

She opened the gate that barred the road, for
there was time, and the children ran across, little
ones hurried by their elders; the gates were closed
again, and they were gone. Soon the company of
little figures was dim upon the distant road like
a flock of sheep in a cloud of dust.

Edwige, with a beating heart, saw the passing
by of the childhood she so longed to cherish.
Turning with her useless love back into the house,

she thought of Lyons, next of Nîmes, and then
of God.

DANIELLE.

The sun is about to rise, and it is hot already.
On all the southward slopes of the hills of La
Corrèze a mist goes up from the grass, the foliage,
the copses heavy with dew. It is the hour when
the cattle must be driven afield. Midway on the
hill-side, nearer to Uzerche than to Brive, a farm
awakes. It is a long, old building, and stands between the fields of maize, of oats, and of potatoes,
and the chestnut woods—the cultivated fields
thrusting their wedges into the domain of the
forest. Lower down are enclosures of clover,
pastures, and a torrent in the valley; and another
hill rises beyond, also with pastures below, with
crops above, with great trees higher still, and with
a summit of bare rocks. The valley is deep, and
the sound of its torrent does not reach the solitary
heights.

Before the farm-house a young man harnessed
his horse to a light carriage, which—his wife
aiding—he then loaded with half-a-dozen little
pigs. This done, the man and woman climbed to
their seats.

"Good-bye, for the present, grandfather,"
cried the man. "Don't expect us before night."

The words were called in the Limousin dialect,
with a sharp note and a singing inflection, and
they still rang against the tiled roof and the window panes when the travellers had swung round to
the back of the farm and begun the descent.

A door opened at the far wing of the building, and a cow walked forth, stretching her neck and snuffing the moist grass, then another cow and then another—seven—and behind the last came the woman who drove them. She was dressed like a beggar, and her feet were in wooden shoes; but under the winged cap of that province her face kept its grave and spiritual beauty. She held, trailing, a long stick cut from a tree and still wearing a few leaves. When she raised her eyes, she looked across at the opposite height.

"Oh, that's you, Danielle; none too soon. In my time the cow-woman was up the hill before sunrise."

"The cows would not be milked," replied Danielle. She added, turning towards the house:

"Good morning, grandfather. Did you sleep well?"

"You know I didn't. I never do. It's a silly question to ask every morning."

The speaker was an old man whose head, in a blue cotton cap, and hairy neck showing in the opening of his shirt, were seen at a narrow window. His rancorous face with its dry, hard wrinkles had little life except in the glances of crimson-lidded eyes. He resumed:

"They are off, those two. You saw them?"

"They are going down the hill now."

"You don't mind being alone. But I can tell you I do."

"Poor grandfather!"

"Don't keep saying 'poor grandfather.' It's all on account of you that I'm in the state I am.

Since you came home from your convent they leave me alone. I am just like a lot of old clothes, chucked into a corner. Nobody as much as thinks of looking at me."

"But don't I take care of you?"

"Your brother did, before you came. And he used to take me to the fairs. I used to have a drink with him. He didn't take his wife. Now that you do her work and he can drive her about, I've got to sit here. You can't say that's not true."

She said nothing.

"Before you came we all got on better. He used to give me money for my tobacco. Sometimes he brought me a hat or a coat. Now I get nothing. I don't know when he means to buy me another pair of shoes, and mine are done for. He just says, 'We've got to keep Danielle.' Well, then, what I say is, you shouldn't have come."

"Where should I have gone?"

"Couldn't you find a place?"

"I tried. I could hear of nothing."

"Couldn't you marry, then?"

"Ah, grandfather!"

"What I say is, you shouldn't have come. It's very hard upon us."

"But you said I might: you called me home."

"I was wrong, then. I thought you would bring back the money."

"What money?"

"The three hundred francs I paid for your clothes when you went."

She walked away hastily, calling, "Good-bye, grandfather. The cows are a long way up."

The reproaches of the old man followed her until she reached a space of silence. She walked up a tree-bordered road, the natural corridor of the forest, a wide path trodden by men and cattle, and barred, at two hundred yards' distance from the farm, by a couple of tall trees. The place looked like a nave with shattered roof, and suggested the recesses of chapels full of shadow. Danielle walked in the middle track, light, erect, and grave. The corn-coloured cattle went on before, wrinkling their hides and swinging their tails under the irritation of the flies. They passed in single file into the wood, crushing the young grass and stirring the branches.

How much altered had Danielle found her old home! Father and mother were dead years ago. The grandfather had grown so old and was so changed that his grandchild hardly knew him again. He was worn, he was unable to work, he was soured by sleeplessness, and yet more by his regrets at an act of his own; he had divided, by deed of gift, his possessions between his sons— the father of Pierre, now master of the farm, and Jacques, who lived nine miles away down the valley. His lamentations over his confined, dependent, hampered, and tedious life never ceased for a day or even an hour. His grandson did not lend an ear to them, nor did that grandson's wife, for these two had ceased to fear him. But in Danielle he had a patient victim. On her he emptied the budget of his complaints and his reproaches. He would willingly have sent her away in the hope of regaining the little presents which he had been used to receive from the master, and which were now economised on the pretext that Danielle was expensive. Now he charged her with laziness, albeit she was the first to rise and the last to rest in that household; and now he returned to the subject of his own privations. He could not see her without a diseased and unreasonable irritation. Nothing soothed him, though Danielle pleaded, met him with patience, and redoubled her attentions to his peevish person. He was well aware that the master and his wife, who had been willing to take into the house for a few weeks this homeless nun, thought with him; her visit was too long; and what if Danielle should ask them some day for her part in the inheritance, voluntarily renounced by her when she entered the religious life? The apprehension was a vain one, but it alarmed those watchful and calculating souls.

Danielle accepted the suspicion, the misjudgment, the insult of her home. She did not even wonder that, violently reproached as she had been for her departure, she should be rebuked for her return. Here, as in the school of Saint Pontique, she was the silent ascetic whose treasure was in the daily cross. She awaited the hour, if such an hour should ever come, when she, like Sister Léonide, might recover in some school a part of that vocation that had been so shattered in the destruction of the convent life.

Since their separation, Danielle had heard oftener than the two others from the old Superior. She was still the counsellor, the trusted one. She knew as well as Sister Justine herself how it was with Léonide and with Edwige. The letters which the postman brought at irregular intervals to the farm were for Danielle an event, a hope, a comfort, but also a cause of keenest griefs. For amid the news, the recollections, the affectionate words, that linked her with one comrade in the mountains of the Ain, and with another in the valley of the Loire, there was often a passage of reference to her who dwelt at Nîmes. And Danielle, always alarmed for that most beloved soul, was anxious, was sorrowful, was fired with the longing to bear the burden of the youngest Sister.

Ah, cruel letters! She kept them hidden in a little wooden box under the mattress of the miserable bed where she lay in the stable—a drover's bed, above the mangers of the cattle and the horses. Cruel letters—she knew their phrases by heart, and pondered them with so keen a compassion that she had no tears left of pity for herself. Dominant love was in her heart; a prevailing resolve that the Kingdom of Heaven should suffer violence on behalf of Pascale. And to-day—for a letter had come on the night preceding—among the high pastures where she kept the cows in solitude, in the sun, in the wind, and in the rain, Danielle prayed, offering her life to God for that Sister whom she was never again to behold on earth.

"*August* 12*th*, 1902.

"And what shall I tell you now of our youngest one? I wish I could write something cheering about that darling of us all, but I cannot. Five days ago came a letter of so worldly a tone that I am more uneasy than ever. Pascale is full of self-congratulation as to the manner in which they treat her at Nîmes. It is evident that she is flattered, that she is indulged and amused, and that her sensibility—the weakness we used to try to cure her of—is worked upon by these people in order to persuade her to accept pleasures not suitable for such as she. She is grateful to them, and bound by her gratitude, with what poor reason you shall judge. She writes, 'You must not be angry, Mother; you must not scold me. It is impossible to refuse when I see how it would hurt them. They are most kind to me, although I see clearly, by many signs, that they are poorer than I thought them. The dress I am wearing— the one that was given to me at Lyons was too hot—they insisted on buying for me. Everything I use they have given me. My aunt never opposes her son when he says that he has planned a walk or an excursion for her and me; and how could I hold back? They give me very little work to do, as they say I am still too weak. Indeed I am, if anything, thinner, in spite of the rest. I still cough a little in the mornings. If I were sure that you were pleased with me, that you did not disapprove, I should be almost quiet in my mind. Quite quiet, quite at peace, I shall never be but at your side.'

"These words of our Pascale will make you as anxious as they have made me. I know little of her surroundings but I feel certain that they are bad for her. I guess many things she does not say. I hope she will say them soon, for I have written her my questions. No one here knows anything of my grief; I think no one would understand it. My poor consumptive boy, whose nurse and companion I am, says to me sometimes: 'What are you thinking about?' And I want to answer: 'About my poor children, who are all so far from me!' Adieu, adieu!

"P.S.—M. Talier-Décapy is dead. That good man, with whom I spoke only once in my life, has left me a legacy. A letter from his lawyer told me of this. I have three thousand francs in the bank. So if you should be in want, let me know."

"October 18th.

"I have had no letter from Pascale since the end of September. I am terribly anxious. Can she be ill? She was in weak health. I hardly dare ask any other question about her. I have written two letters since her last, the second one very urgent, both very affectionate. No answer. I wrote—though rather reluctantly— to her aunt Prayou. She has made no reply. I cannot rest in this state of doubt—I am too unhappy. You must advise me. This is what I have done so far: Do you remember a girl called Louise Casale, who was friendly to our school? Her family were Nîmes people. She

was an anæmic girl, and had been to the lay
school, and she used to come to see us. She
was not ignorant of the world, but quite good
and innocent at heart. I asked this Louise to
help me. 'Try to think,' I wrote to her, 'of
some relation of yours at Nîmes, or some friend,
someone to be trusted, who can find out and
tell me what has happened to my child, whether
for good or ill.' I am still waiting. And I am
sorry, I accuse myself, I often cry bitterly, for
having, at a time of hard trouble, allowed this
poor little Pascale to leave me; I ought to have
kept her, at any cost—of hard work, of poverty,
of cold, of death itself. I should have saved
her. Where is she now? Pray for us both,
Danielle."

"November 3rd.

"My Sister Danielle,—Our darling whom we
all loved, who had nothing against her but the
weakness ·of her gentle heart, who had taken
refuge amongst us, whom we are no longer able
to protect—I cannot write the words without
tears. Sister Danielle, she has allowed herself
to be deceived; she has thought herself in love;
she has fallen from God. I cannot doubt it.
I learnt it yesterday from a relative of Louise
Casale, a widow—Madame Rioul, who lives at
Montauri. This woman knew nothing of the
history of our child, but she perceived the temptation and the persuasion. It was always so easy
to persuade Pascale; she yielded so readily to a
kind word; she thought their love was good and

innocent. They flattered her, amused her, bound
her by their attentions and their presents, until
she was at their mercy. They were each other's
accomplices, these people, mother and son. They
are suspected and feared where they live. Not
only is the mother unable to restrain the worst
actions of her son, she has served her own vile
interests. She knew that in this girl, whom she
allowed to be corrupted, she would have an unpaid
servant compelled to stay in the house. Pascale
fallen, my Danielle! Pascale, almost a saint,
given over to brute beasts! How she will suffer!
Far more than those would who were not called
to a consecrated life. All day long I have thought
I heard her cry for help. Is it true, is it true that
she is lost?"

"*November* 8th.

"You say 'Go to her, speak to her, take her
away.' Do you suppose I did not immediately
think of that? Should I be her mother if I did
not think of it? The widow, Madame Rioul,
tried gently to speak to Pascale, and was repulsed.
But she is not I. When I first heard the dreadful
news, six days ago, I tried to get away. I went
to Madame de Roinnet in her room to ask for leave.
Of course, I could not give her my reasons. She
was much distressed. She said: 'If you leave us,
even for one day, I cannot answer for the conse-
quences. You have been here only three months
and you want a holiday already! M. de Roinnet
will take advantage of your going to discharge you
altogether, and what will become of us without

you?' I was going to say: 'All the same, I must go,' when Guy rushed in; he had been listening. He had a terrible attack. I was obliged to attend to him only. So then I took advice of a confessor. He said: 'Do not give up a clear and certain duty of charity for a mission too likely to fail. The hour is not yet come when you will be heard by her whom you go to seek. When she is able to come to you, you will hear her cries and her tears. Wait!' So I am waiting, but I can hardly live in such torment of mind. My thoughts are not here; they are all with her who is unworthy."

"*November 22nd.*

"I have another letter from Nîmes, but not from Pascale. But first of all, forgive me. I used too hard a word. Unworthy she may be. But you have thought, as I have, of all the things that lighten her sin. She did not seek evil, she was thrown into it. Iniquitous laws cast her into the peril from which she had fled. She has been the poor quarry that dogs and huntsmen drive from its cover to the guns.

"She is guilty, but the Judge who cannot be deceived will surely not punish her. She had a credulous heart, she was easily touched, she was a most grateful creature. And by these sweet characters they have caught her, and keep her captive! She had no mother; no doubt she thought she had found a real home, a real family, at Nîmes. She went there in obedience to me, her Superior. The gentle Pascale had to defend herself against a man well versed in the art of overcoming women, a handsome man, I am told, a cunning one, cruel under an attractive surface, and a cleverer talker than anyone in Lyons. And she was young, and they lived in the same house.

"I will not repeat to you the details that have been told me. You can guess them. It is only the story of a common seduction. You visited with me the unhappy ones of the Lyons streets. The frightful thing is that this is Pascale, and that we cannot help her."

"Sunday, January 18th, 1903.

"They tell me that she hardly ever speaks, that she is gloomy and angry, she who was so joyous. No one in the Montauri district knows what a blessed calling was hers, or what a blessed creature she was. Jules Prayou has taken care that no one shall know. The indifferent, the impious even, would think such a fall too cruel a scandal. I hear that Pascale is closely watched, closely kept, and hardly ever leaves the house; the time of excursions and fairs and walks and presents is long gone by."

"February.

"Our child is more helpless than ever. Prayou has left her for other women. She is his mother's servant, and does all the work of the house, earning only contempt, unpitied and silent. She has not given her confidence to anyone, and no one sees her cry. If she would only speak, and call me!

Has she not suffered enough to make her call me yet, or has she suffered too much? Who can tell me?"

"Friday, March 27th.

"The neighbours say that the man often insults her and beats her. And yet the time has not yet come. Madame Rioul met her four days ago in the street and said to her, 'You look ill.' Pascale answered: 'If I do, whose business is it?' The widow said: 'It is the business of those who wish you well, as I do, Madame Pascale, and as Sister Justine does.' Pascale was pale, and turned her head away. She said: 'I don't know what you mean.'"

Other fragments of letters during the spring and early summer had brought to Danielle a renewal of sorrow. Then, suddenly, at the end of July, a desperate word had come from Justine. The night before that serene sunrise on the forest of Corrèze, Danielle had received these hurried lines:

"I am leaving for Nîmes. My child has not called me, but I know now that she has been brought to the lowest of all disgrace. She is a slave, she is his property. I must set her free. For two days, Danielle, think of nothing, pray for nothing, else. JUSTINE."

In the forest, following her cows, walks Danielle. It has not been necessary to bid her think of nothing else. No other thought, no other image,

goes up with her into the solitude of the mountain.
The path grows steep, it passes between rocks
overturned, the trees grow fewer, and the oldest
lift up heads ruined by storms. Danielle, all
alone with God, walks with her arms out in the
form of a cross, praying like Joan of Domrémy,
like Germaine, like Geneviève. Now and then a
square rock between two chestnut trees, standing
in the sunrise, has the aspect of an altar.

V.

PASCALE.

IT was nine o'clock, and the night was hot; hotter still the dusty breath of the city of Nîmes. The soil gave back the heat of the day; and the odour of the gutters, of the cellars, of the houses, of the manure dropped by the carts and crushed by their wheels, of the melon peel and other refuse of fruit lying about the doors—all rose together into the weary air. On the hills beyond, a western breeze carried scents of lavender, of rosemary, of mint, and of foliage and thirsty plants. In the streets there was hardly air enough to stir the stale and heavy odours, but when a little motion came all who felt it were glad to be out of doors. The people of Nîmes—those whom the hot weather had not driven out of town—walked to and fro, drank in the cafés, the wine-shops, and the inns, strolled round the fountains, and sat wherever they found a bench.

At the head of the wide Cours de la République, where lie the fountain gardens, the working-men and shop-people passed and repassed slowly, chatting, well pleased, their work over. There was a good deal of laughter. Many girls paraded a fancied beauty. Love intrigues, jokes, small slanders, filled all these minds and made all the talk.

No grave thought came by; one might easily count the faces that looked even slightly serious. Many children were led up and down in the evening air. Soldiers were loitering or going back to barracks. Aloft, beyond the street and above the pine-wood, the Magne tower stood up like a lighthouse, vague and extinct in the night.

A woman stood motionless near the row of nettle trees, and leant against a gas-lamp. The shadow of the base of the gas-jet fell over her, wavering. Her trade was to be guessed by the signs of her youth, her solitude, and her taking no part in the movement around her. She had her back to the fluctuating crowd. She knew that those who wanted her would come to her. But from time to time her eyes turned askance towards one group among the townspeople. This group was formed by a young man, slender, young, well dressed, wearing a straw hat and a scarf-pin; by a younger man, with a long, southern body and short legs, and by two women. The man walked to and fro in the lights, narrowing his eyes now and then to make out the thin form of the solitary girl under the lamp-post. He talked continuously, with his customary gesticulation and recurring laughter. At times his eyes and hers met sidelong, and the brief exchange of glances made the woman rigid again. She was afraid.

This was her third night on that pavement. She was a thing to be used, with no right of complaint. As the man bade her, she waited in the street, the butt of the contemptuous jokes of the passers by, or the object of their random

desires; she had no will, no choice, no name.
When the shadow flickered from her bare head,
it might be seen that she had beautiful fair hair,
thick but short, so that it made a small flat knot
behind.

A man lounging on a seat at a couple of yards'
distance caught sight of her, looked again, and
stood up. He lurched towards her, and she drew
away, slipping behind the lamp-post. The man
came on with his arms out, steadying himself.
He wore the dress of the drovers of the Cevennes,
who bring their herds and flocks to the market at
Nîmes. His square, coarse face, framed in short
whiskers, wore a fixed laugh, and between his fat,
earthen-coloured cheeks showed the edges of strong
teeth. The girl would have eluded him, but
for the young man watching; she was afraid.
Even so, as she drew back out of the uncertain
shadow into the light beyond, she was more
easily seen: she was sweet, she was delicate, she
was ashamed, she was afraid. For fear that the
drover might take her hands, she thrust them
into the pockets of her blue apron. This scene of
misery, of sensible and conscious shame, came to
pass in the open street amid the voices, the dust,
the indifference, or the curiosity of the strolling
crowd. The man groped, came against the lamp-
post, grasped it, drew up his great stature, and
with his free hand seized the woman and dragged
her to him to kiss her. She struggled, uttering a
momentary cry. There was some laughter among
the crowd because here was a harlot who would
not be kissed. Someone cried, "Hold on!" A

police agent looked on from a distance. A
drunkard rather rough with a wanton—it was
common, it was normal. There was nothing for
the police to do. From a group that had stopped
the young man in the straw hat stepped hastily,
and came close to the woman.

"Come," he said in a low voice, "take him
home; or must I make you?"

She looked with terror in the speaker's face.
She still struggled feebly against the drover, who
held her now by the wrists.

"You won't do as I tell you?" whispered the
young man, who was twirling his watch, with the
chain twisting round his fingers, "We'll settle
that by and bye. Take him home now, and be
quick!"

Suddenly she succeeded in getting her wrists
free by a wrench, turned, and ran towards the
Cadereau. A few cheers followed her, but she
had not run twenty paces when the drover
caught her by the arm. Together they turned
off the Cours de la République into one of the side
streets of the workmen's quarter. The young
man, who had also turned to follow, came back;
and one of the two women walking with him
watched the fragile and captive figure as it passed
out of sight, and said to him with a laugh:

"You've got trouble at home, I see."

"Yes, I've had it for a day or two. It's not
going to last, though. I shall take care of
that." And he struck his fist into his own left
hand.

The hot night dried still further the dry streets,

the people came and went, seeking the open ways and hoping for a wandering breeze.

*　　*　　*　　*　　*　　*

It was five o'clock, and the summer morning was limpid. The door of the Prayous' cottage, on the waste land, opened to give egress to the feeble figure of a woman who leant against the door-post as though she had turned faint in the fresh air. But there was no wind, and the day would soon be burning. The woman wore her last night's dress, but on her shoulders was a little shawl that fell loose on either side. Pale she was and thin, and in her face was no pleasure at the beauty of the summer morning; her eyes were entirely sad. She pushed before her a wheelbarrow loaded with a great pile of linen under a sheet. As she paused to shut the door behind her, her eyes ranged over all the windows of the neighbouring houses. All the women, all the people behind those windows, laughed at her, she thought. They were tenants of the Prayous; they used to bow to her—Madame Rioul, Madame Lantosque, Madame Cabeirol, and the rest, and their husbands, their brothers, their lovers; and the Mayols —the husband, the wife, the sister, who lived opposite; they all laughed at her now; they knew things about her. They had seen her going down all those months. They must have heard her cry out in the night, when Jules Prayou came home at two o'clock and beat her; when he ran after her up the stairs; when she opened the window screaming for help. No doubt they were

watching her now from behind some shutter.
That widow Rioul, who went out working by the
day—who was respectable, and boasted of it, she
was old. But the tailor's wife in the same house,
she had been talked about, pretty things were said
of her. She read cheap novels all day, and one
could see it in her face. As to the Cabeirols, the
little tramway employé and his wife, who had
taken the house to the left, what had they to say
about her? People who had not paid a penny
of rent for six months! They might be quiet,
at any rate, and not show how they despised
her. Ah! if she had someone to protect her—
to protect her? She needed to be loved. But
there was no one now to love Pascale.

She took up her burden, crossed the waste
land, and reached the road leading down to the
torrent. The neighbours had not yet unclosed
their shutters. One man only was watering his
garden. Beyond the bridge, on the quay, very
few shops were open. a wine-shop or two, and
here or there a provision shop for the country
people. No one was yet at the public washing-
tank, roofed with tiles, by the bridge. So much
the better. She unloaded her barrow, rolled up
her sleeves, knelt at the nearest place by the
long basin, and turned the tap by means of
which the rushing stream kept those useful waters
flowing. A woman passed down the road in a
little clanking cart full of milk cans; she did not
turn her head towards the tank, and took no
notice of the girl who was beginning to wash the
household linen of Madame Prayou. A long train

of dust followed the cart. Pascale dipped her
linen, soaped it, beat it with the wooden beater,
but was obviously unable to work long; after
five painful minutes she stopped, closed her eyes,
and hung crouching on her heels, with her arms
on the cement edging the tank, and her fingers
in the running water. The sun began to burn on
the tiled roof; the shadows of the houses by the
waterside grew shorter and became filled with
reflected light.

Little was left of the aspect of that Pascale
who thirteen months before had journeyed to
Nîmes in search of what she needed—protection.
Her credulity, her imprudence, a pleasant remembrance still sounding in her heart of youth,
had brought her to these two enemies. They had
made haste to corrupt her, and with how many
accomplices! The loss of the example of her
companions; the loss of that religious Rule which
not only directed the will but practised it, so that
by the deliberate election of every hour of the day
it grew in force and dominance over self; the loss
of the tender, the pure, the intelligent love of her
Sisters; grief for the destruction of the life she
had chosen and of the work that made life worth
while—all these things served the purpose of
Jules Prayou. He had received her with respect
and reserve; he had kept the secret of her past
which she wished to mourn over alone as another
woman would guard the memory of disappointed
love; he had taken her part against the preju-
dice of the grudging neighbours, slow to admit a
stranger; and he had given her—unused to pos-

sess anything—presents that to her, poor girl,
seemed noble. By degrees, yet soon enough, she
had been undone. Brief was her error, but it
could not be effaced. On the morrow the sense
of the irreparable grasped her; it had never again
let her go. It came with the first remorse; it
turned repentance to despair. It was now all-
dominant.

"How did I fall?" she said throughout the
miserable days. "Unhappy Pascale! To have
been what I have been, to be what I am. To
have had that mother, that dear father, the
companionship of saints! To have been honoured,
respected, cherished, and now to have to avoid
the eyes of all chaste women! To have been an
elect one, to be a traitress! Well did I know—a
girl of eighteen—my own weakness. My call to
the life of the cloister was only distrust of myself,
with which He whom I can no longer name had
been good enough to mingle a little love of divine
things. All is over and done, all is wrecked. The
only future I hoped for is barred. Even if better
things came again, and the convents were opened,
and the nuns went back, there would never,
never, never be any place for me. Who would
let me teach little girls how to be good and to
resist temptation? I am down, and I shall never
rise. I am the condemned one for ever, for ever;
I am the lost one."

Soon, too, she had tasted the bitterness of the
full knowledge of the plot against her. Brief
had been the illusion of love; she was hated,
not loved. And she knew that mother and son

had worked together for her fall. She was the
mother's servant, and in a more terrible sense
the slave of the son. When the time was ripe
he would use his power over her beauty and her
youth to the utmost, to the last, to the lowest.
He was a needy man, and she was to make money
for him. She attempted a last resistance. She
wished to kill herself, but she was a lost soul and
in mortal fear of the grave. That at least must
be put off. Could she fly from the hateful house?
Jules Prayou had taken means to hold her.

Of all she said, of all she did, he was apprised.
Pascale felt herself surrounded by a network of
treason. Her master was a man to be feared,
and many did fear him. This young man,
without avowable means of life, without reputa-
tion, and without work, had innumerable accomplices, had surrounded himself with con-
nivances. He held the district—not only the
suburb of Montauri, but the neighbourhood of
the slaughter-houses, and all the region of the
cattle and sheep market. Though he took no
open part in politics, several political agents
paid him a covert court. They said: "It is
not a good thing to have Prayou against us."
At election time he was flush of money. The
very police agents who had been charged to
keep a watch on him had entered into treaty
with him—the man of whom all crime was suspected and no crime known. With him they
could enter into doubtful wine-shops where he
was all-powerful, could drink without payment,
and Jules Prayou helped them in inquisitions

they could not entirely evade. At this price he purchased liberty from surveillance for himself. Smugglers of alcohol made use of his experience and of his knowledge of men and places; poachers found him an expert middle-man. The owners of olive-orchards knew that for a fee to him they would be tolerably well guaranteed against thieves; at any rate, the whole of their crop would not disappear. When the tall young fellow with the soft dark eyes walked through the district all saluted him on the way, and many hats, even, were raised. He answered with a word or with a sweep of the eyelid, according to the importance of the case. Women looked at him. Newspaper-sellers left the pavement to him; the gypsies, who kept their tribe close, gave him welcome to their camp; wandering musicians and all kinds of beggars, true and false alike, tried to get his favour. And all these people kept him informed. They said: "I saw your girl at the fountain garden. I saw her on the Saint Césaire road." Nor did Pascale ever go out without leave or without a time fixed for her return.

She was indeed the slave, longing to revolt, but held in deadly fear. She had grown so pallid and was so wasted that the neighbours said, "What a face! She won't last long at this rate." She never saw Prayou but a nervous trembling seized her; at times it did not leave her for hours. She had her cough; she often felt feverish; she had frequent painful languor in her limbs. Her faltering blood left her helpless against her tyrant.

But immeasurably more dreadful was the dis-

tress of her soul, for here was indeed despair.
She fought away her memories ten times, twenty
times, a hundred times; they returned: at daybreak, at dusk, at the mid-day bells, in those
moments of respite that would formerly have
been filled with peace. At the suggestion of a
face or the sound of a voice the idea came in spite
of her:

"Getting-up time—Sister Léonide is pulling
the bell. The Angelus—we are going across to
the church. Now it is the meditation. The
sun is setting—the little girls are gone. Edwige,
my beloved! Sister Danielle! And you on whom
we all depended—our Mother, Justine! Oh, the
horror! Oh, the profanation! I never will see
you again. Keep away from my pit, you holy
ones, keep away!"

All was gone, all was lost—liberty, the light
heart, even the beauty and brightness of those
eyes, those golden eyes, where the look of youth
was quenched. All had changed except something of her love of children. She had been so
fond of them, their confidence, their kisses.

What a weight of grief she must put aside so
that she might work to-day. Work, for what?
for whom?

The morning was wearing on; all the shops
were open; the nets were hung out before their
doors to keep off the flies. Pascale made another
effort, raised her head, and resumed her washing
of the linen she had left steeping in the tank.
A black figure coming from the bridge darkened
the sunshine for a moment and passed on. It was

the widow Rioul with her air of ladylike poverty.
She went out early for her work in two households,
and was also accustomed to hear daily mass at
St. Paul's. She had not seen Pascale, it seemed.
In any case, she went her way, the edge of her
black dress already white with dust. Since the
day, now some months ago, when she had ventured to warn Pascale, "I advise you to be careful, Mademoiselle; people are talking about you,"
and had been repulsed, the old woman had not
spoken to her. She crossed the open space
beyond the tank and disappeared into the streets.
The cigalas were many and noisy. The woman
at her washing unfastened the neck of her blue
bodice, for the heat. She heard voices coming
down the hill from Montauri, young voices that
she knew, and she named the speakers to herself
as they drew near: Marie Lantosque, a tenant of
the Prayous; Madame Mayol, who lived opposite;
and her sister, a young girl who was about to be
married. The three women crossed the bridge,
and as they passed the tank they turned to Pascale
without stopping: "Good morning," they cried,
in patois, "Good morning, Madame Pascaù! It
will be hot enough in another hour."

They were laughing together, and Pascale followed them with her eyes, wringing her linen with
her two weary hands. "They spoke to me," she
thought, "they don't want to show too clearly how
they despise me. But what are they thinking
about me all the time? Madame Lantosque
seemed to be mocking me, I thought."

She suffered as she invented a conversation

among the three. She had so lost reasonable
control that she began to fight with her work,
beating the linen in a bitter and helpless rage.
For a time anger gave her strength. To have
done—to have done with it all—that was her
impotent desire. And as she worked, exhausting
herself, a child, a light, a joy, came under the
shadow of the roof. It was little Delphine
Cabeirol, whom they called Finette, a girl of ten,
gay, spirited, with sombre, long hair and lovely
eyes, green as olives, and full of childish surprise.
Why had she come? She went leaping down the
passage where the places are set for the women
to kneel at their work, holding a little parcel in her
hand; suddenly, seeing the neighbour, the woman
to whom her mother had forbidden her to speak,
she stopped. She was embarrassed, and began to
unknot her bundle quietly, keeping her head down.
Madame Pascale was so busy beating and soap-
ing and dipping that perhaps she had not seen
her. No, she had paused in her labour; and the
eyes that should have been so soft dwelt upon her.
Madame Pascale withdrew her hands from the
water, and let them rest on her wet apron. She
knelt, her thin figure slightly towards Delphine,
but did not smile as women do when they want
a kiss from a child; nevertheless, in her sad face
was an urgent invitation. Both were so quiet that
the humming mosquitoes made more noise than
they. Pascale looked timorous, as though she
might frighten the girl away—as one watches a
bird. And it was Delphine who spoke first when
she saw tears coming into the eyes she met. Her

little things were before her, and a large lump
of soap. She was rather a Provençale than a
Nîmoise, and she used the gentle, old-fashioned
Provençale salutation as she said:

"Good morning, Madame Pascale. I have
brought these things for my mother, and she is
coming too." She bowed her clear, pale face,
which rose again like the ivory key of a piano, and
was about to go.

"Tell me, Delphine, have you had leave to
speak to me this morning?"

"No," said the child, over her shoulder.

"Then you saw I was unhappy, and that was
why you said 'Good morning,' was it?"

Delphine looked "yes."

"I guessed that was why. I know little girls—
I used to know them so well. You are quite right
if you think I am unhappy. I am very unhappy."

The beautiful large olive-coloured eyes were
veiled with feeling.

"Everyone is very wicked to me, Delphine.
Will you be kind, little Delphine?"

The child twisted her hands uneasily, and again
looked what she did not speak. "What do you
want me to do? It makes me unhappy too to
see you so dreadfully sad, and I don't understand—. If you want me to do something I can
do without being too disobedient—I will be a
little disobedient if you like."

"I only want you to come and kiss me, little
Delphine. No, no. I don't mean that. Give
me your hand, just your hand, will you? It
would do me good. Nobody loves me."

The child smiled. Was that all? She came, with her two hands out, to be kissed. But before she reached Pascale, she halted, listened, skipped on her light feet, and fled.

"There's mother," she said, and in three bounds she was at the other end of the passage, then on the sunny road. Pascale heard some rapid words in dialect between Delphine, who was defending herself, and her mother, who was chiding; and Madame Cabeirol entered. She shifted her child's things so that she should be further away from "that creature." Nevertheless, she said as the others had done, "Good morning, Madame Pascale," but spoke the words hurriedly and low, so that Pascale did not hear them. She was a Provençale of the small, dry, thin and vivid type. She felt herself, as a married woman, much superior to Pascale. She disapproved of the disorderly life of the Prayous, and their extravagant expenditure, with an entirely human disapproval, unconnected with religion. But she made no show of it, being a tenant of the Prayous, and a tenant much in arrears with the rent. She would have cut the neighbourhood long since, she said, if the times had not been so bad with Cabeirol. Even so, she would have to go some day soon, on account of her girl, who was sharp and forward, and who would soon understand what was going on. Meantime, until her husband got a better place with the tramway company, she must put up with it, but it would be pleasant to have more respectable neighbours. She knelt down and began to rub, to beat, and to soap, as Pascale was doing. And Pascale, angry at the child's flight, took no notice of her. She had straightened her own dress with a hasty hand. This woman must indeed despise her, to forbid a child of ten to speak to her. "Cruel, cruel! Why should one woman so insult another? one woman so fortunate as she," thought Pascale, "and another so unhappy as I. If she could see something beyond the life I am leading, if she could see my heart, and the infinite disgust, and the loathing—what am I thinking of? If she knew what I really am, what I was, she would despise me more than she does a hundred times. She would hold my head under that water and drown me, and put an end to me."

The two women worked. The sun, reflected from the bright white road and from the water in the basin, lighted their worn faces from below. Madame Cabeirol's was lined by poverty, faded by years of hard life, ill nourished. Pascale's showed the clear signs of disease; there was an ominous transparence in her white cheek, in the delicate ears that might have been those of an alabaster statue, and in her hands that looked so slender in the running water.

A few people passed by. The noise of the streets went on; mothers were heard calling their children into the shade.

Pascale's arms grew lax. She coughed, with a little dry cough, as though her chest lacked strength for a greater effort. Then suddenly she fell back on her heels, her breast rising, her nostrils blue and dilated, her eyes fixed and full of anguish. In a few moments she leaned her shoulder against the wall at her side. Madame Cabeirol finished her wringing of Delphine's little nightgowns, because it is not good manners to take any notice of people, if they are not one's own relations, at such times as these. After a while, however, she glanced at Pascale, for the fit had passed and the girl was setting to work again, gathering the clothes she had washed, to take them away for drying. Then pity spoke; for her neighbour was obviously exhausted. The woman was impulsive, and it vexed her to see even those she disliked suffer beyond a certain degree of pain.

"Oh," she said, "are you not ill, Madame Pascale?"

Pascale replied: "What does it matter to you? Ill or not, I've got to go on."

Madame Cabeirol's compassion was proof against the hard answer, and she said:

"I might help you to put your things to dry. I have very little to do this morning as it happens. I've done already."

She showed her heap of clean linen.

"I am not used to being helped," said Pascale, "but if you have time to waste you can do as you like."

Madame Cabeirol left her place, and began to pile the chemises and shirts, handkerchiefs, towels and petticoats that Pascale had washed. Rather stupefied than touched, Pascale watched her, wondering why she did it. She stood idle—it was enough labour to draw her breath. The

silence at last irritated Madame Cabeirol's nerves,
and she said snappishly:

"All the same, your being in trouble is no reason
for treating people as though they were dogs, is it?"

"Trouble?" said Pascale, turning her eyes on
her neighbour's face. "What do you know about
my trouble?"

"Do you suppose I can't guess it pretty well?
A young thing like you shouldn't look so unhappy
as you do."

Pascale kept the hard aspect she had, but she
seemed to listen. It was the first time anyone
had had compassion upon her since the day on
which she had come beneath the roof of Jules
Prayou. Four old laundry-women by profession,
all talking, came in at that moment and took their
customary places.

"At your age," continued Madame Cabeirol,
coming close, with her dark, quick, vivacious head
close to the fair abandoned young head of Pascale.
"At your age, and with your looks—you've got
some good looks left, you know—ought you to let
them treat you as they do?"

"You heard, then, last night, or the other
nights?"

"Suppose I did. He beat you, didn't he?"

"Yes, he beat me."

"You know it's not nice—it's a bad business
—what he makes you do, I mean. I may not
be exactly religious, and I allow that a woman
has a right to do what she chooses with her own
body. But all the same, if you were married to
him, he would have to treat you better."

Pascale recoiled.

"Married to someone else, then, Madame
Pascale. Not to him if you don't like him.
Don't get angry. You would get some one easily
enough. Now, look at me——"

Pascale seized her arm. "Never to him, never
to any other, never!"

"Not married already, are you?"

"No, no."

"Well, then?"

Pascale made an effort, took up some of the
linen, and said:

"Don't mind me. I can't get rid of my trouble.
I brought it on myself, and when one does that,
one has to suffer, that's all. One has to die,
anyway. Yes, help me to put out my things to
dry, if you will be so kind. It's all you can do
for me."

The woman stood up, saying under her breath:

"I should run away—wouldn't I run?—if
Cabeirol so much as lifted a hand——"

The two women went out together, each carrying an armful of white linen, and on the rounded
top of the long, low wall that skirts the stream
they spread it to the sun. All white things in that
light—the whitewash of the walls, even the white
pebbles in the water, seemed to flame and shine.
Dust rose here and there apparently without any
wind. A wild impulse seemed to carry it upwards.
All things that live for light were full of their joy
—flies of all sorts and sizes, innumerable cigalas
and grass-hoppers by the stream-side. Eleven
o'clock had struck some time since. A few chil-

dren were straggling up the hill towards Montauri,
and, more slowly after them, men and women
weary with their hot morning in the work-rooms.

Down the hill came one woman, a stranger.
She walked from Montauri towards the city.
She wore a clumsy and shabby black woollen
dress, heavy, horribly hot. In spite of the heat,
and in spite of the sweat that bathed her face,
she had a little black veil. As she came near the
bridge she met Madame Cabeirol, now empty-
handed.

"Will you give me some information I want,
dear lady?" asked the stranger.

"At your service," replied the thin Provençale,
peering through the veil.

"You may know a woman named Pascale
Mouvand?"

"Mouvand? I can't say. People round here
would be more likely to call her Pascale Prayou,"
said the woman, with a laugh.

The other did not laugh. She said: "That is
the person I am in search of. I have just come
from the house where she lives. They told me
she was washing at the tank. Is that true?"

"There she is," said Madame Cabeirol, pointing
to the women at work. "That is the one, just
stooping now to pick up some more of her things.
Shall I call her?"

"Oh, no; oh, no! Wait a little."

The Provençale was surprised at the emotion
caused by those simple words. The stranger
grasped at her own throat as though she could
hardly get her breath, trying the while to make

out the figure she sought, at some twenty yards' distance, under the tiled roof. But she shook her head.

"My eyes," she said, "are not very good today. I can't see her. Will you tell her that one of her friends is here and wants her? I shall wait behind this wall, by the bridge."

She walked on into the secluded space formed by the parapets of the torrent and the bridge, and by the wall enclosing the washing-place, while Madame Cabeirol went in. Two minutes had hardly passed. The noise of the beating of the linen went on steadily, and the women were chattering without a pause; through all sang the fresh and clear voice of the running water. In the great vast sunshine waited the stranger in black, hearing nothing, conscious of but one thought, one name, one image, one appeal, and all was gathered up in one prayer—"Ave Maria." It was never finished. She whom she sought and desired came out, and seeing the stranger, whose veil still left her face recognisable, knowing her, knowing her one friend, her mother, cried out like a child in terror. Her eyes dilated with a look of anguish. She fell back against the wall, her hands flat against its face.

"You, you!" she panted; and the old woman, with infinite and immeasurable love, called her, very low, very low, by the old name:

"Sister Pascale?"

She drew near to the lost one, she held forth those familiar arms. But Pascale pushed her off and hid her head in her hands.

"No, don't come near me.   Go away, go away!"

"Pascale, I know you are unhappy. I have come to take you away."

"Don't speak to me. Go away. You don't know, you don't know what I am."

"I do know. You are my Pascale."

"I am not. I am another creature. I am something else. You can't take me back. I am damned, I am cursed. Go away!"

She was crushing her bare face, her bare arms, against the wall.

Sister Justine touched her shoulder.

"I want you to come, in the sacred name of the Mercy that has sent me."

"No, never."

"I shall take you by force."

"No—no."

Pascale ran out into the road. But the old woman caught her, seized her by the wrist, drew her to her breast, held her there, and when she felt the fair head stuggled no more, but lay hidden on her shoulder, she said:

"Pascale, all our Sisters have prayed for you. Sister Danielle has suffered."

She stopped for an answer, and could hear stifled words more painful to listen to than cries, and more heart-piercing:

"I can't, I can't be saved."

"Pascale, Sister Léonide is working for you."

Pascale spoke no more, but tried to wrench herself from those maternal arms. Desperately Justine pleaded again:

"Pascale, your own Sister Edwige is undergoing a martyrdom for you. She offers it for you. It is

she who urged me to come. You must not with-
stand her; let her save you."

Pascale, half-hidden in the old Sister's cloak,
ceased to strain against her arms.

"Take me away, then," she whispered at last.

Sister Edwige had won. The absent ones
were there. Pascale raised her head, as though
regaining her hold on life after delirium, put her
hand to her disordered hair, glancing furtively
between her fingers to see if anyone were looking.
There were witnesses: workmen, shopmen from
the quay, the women from the tank, and all
watched with keen curiosity these two—one of
them a stranger, who had seemed to be quarrelling
with the girl, and then had followed that close
embrace.

"Oh," said Pascale, "how difficult it will be
to get away! and all the linen out there, and
Madame Cabeirol who will ask where I am going,
and the others——"

She was pulling down her sleeves mechanically.
Sister Justine straightened her old cloak.

"Come, child," she repeated, "come!"

They left the place. Sister Justine had Pascale's arm under hers. Pascale was now weeping, in spite of herself—people were looking at
her. They were saying: "What is the matter
with her? Why is she going? Who is the old
woman?"

"Come quicker," said Justine.

The groups parted to let them pass, and their
feet were on the pavement of the road when
Pascale heard a man running.

"There he is," she panted; "it is all over; I am lost. Run away, Mother, run away!"

The old name of mother had broken from her heart. Sister Justine turned and placed Pascale behind her.

"Don't, don't," said Pascale, "go no nearer. He might kill you."

Jules Prayou, by an authoritative gesture, called up the spectators. They came running, as though bidden by him to a show. He wore his insolent air, his hard look, his false composure. His jaw was twisted with anger. He went close to Pascale, taking no notice of the old woman who covered her.

"Go home!" he ordered. "You were running away, were you? You shall see what comes of that. Go home, do you hear me?"

He pointed the way. Sister Justine pressed forward, her large courageous face defying him.

"Go home yourself!" she said.

"And why, pray?"

"Because I am taking her away."

Prayou scanned her.

"You are, old woman? And who may you be?"

"I am her mother."

"That is not true; she has no mother."

"I hold that place. And you, then, what are you?"

"I am her lover."

"Go, get yourself another mistress, then; this one is going."

"You thief, I'll stop you!" cried the man.

"Go for the police!" shouted Sister Justine. "Help us, all good people!"

Heads appeared at the windows. A group of masons who were lunching in a tavern ran out eating their bread. They saw a shabby woman, much embarrassed by her clothes, out of breath, flushed, opposing foot to foot the great Prayou, the king of the suburb. They saw him put her aside with a single turn of his hand and catch by the arms, close under the shoulders, the ashen-pale and shuddering Pascale, who was straining her head back, recoiling from him. They were inclined, somewhat timidly, to take the woman's part.

"Come, don't hurt the girl, Monsieur Prayou," said someone. "Let the woman speak. Don't hold the girl in that way, or she may faint. She is free, after all, like the rest of us."

"Free, is she? Who said that?" cried Prayou, turning his head to search the crowd with his eyes, but keeping his hold.

The crowd was willing to hear. The old stranger, parted from Pascale, tried in vain to reach her again.

"You see that old thief who has been to my house," said Prayou's dominant voice, "and who has come down here to get this girl. Go and fetch the police—that's just what I want you to do. Pascale will say whether she wants to stay with me or not. Answer, Pascale!"

He dug with his fingers between the muscles of her arms. She pulled back, with her look of terror, but said nothing. The crowd repeated louder, "Let her go, then, let her go!"

"You do want to stay? Say so!" repeated the man over the convulsed face of Pascale. "A girl who is my own relative, whom I took in when she had not a penny, whom I have kept ever since—come, tell them you want to stay," he said again.

The pale lips answered at last:

"No, I don't. I want to go with Sister Justine."

A cry rose from the crowd: "Poor girl, poor girl! Hear what she says!"

Sister Justine strove to speak. The crowd was divided in opinion. "He is right." "No, no. The girl has a right to go!" Women were crying out, raising clenched fists. Then Prayou, lifting his lofty head, cried louder than the clamour:

"I'll have you to know the whole story. You see that old woman. She is out of her convent; she was a nun, and Pascale was another. The Government set this girl free, and the old woman wants to force her back to a nunnery. Now, friends, her nunnery is in my house, and I mean to take her home."

He stooped, took Pascale under the knees and round the waist, and carried her off like a sack, for she had lost consciousness. The crowd parted for him, and closed again around Sister Justine.

"Settle that woman's business!" he cried to them, over his shoulder.

Followed by one or two women, he strode towards Montauri, up the road that led home. Behind him he heard the noise of the crowd that was hustling the woman in mourning, assailing her with the name of thief and ex-nun, pushing

her towards the street, and remembering—some
of them—the denunciations of convents which
they had heard at anti-clerical meetings; these
insulted, in the person of the stranger, her religious past.

Jules Prayou went home with his burden,
pushed open the door, traversed the corridor,
the feet and the skirt of Pascale grazing the wall
as he went.

"What are you carrying? What, Pascale?
Has she had an accident? What's the matter?"

His mother was still screaming after him when
he was at the other side of the court, under his
own roof, in the little building that looked on the
waste land. He was tottering and exhausted.
His foot struck the second of the two doorsteps,
and he was nearly thrown down. Exasperated,
alone, without witnesses, he lifted with a last effort
of his strength the body of the girl and hurled it
violently against the wall where the stairs began.
Her head and her bosom struck the wall, then the
helpless figure fell upon the boards, heaped upon
the lowest stair, the feet on the threshold.

She was conscious, but she had not screamed;
she groaned once, and then made no more sound,
and moved no more. Her face was in the shadow,
turned to the wall. A thread of blood crept from
her mouth. Prayou stooped to look, and called
to his mother, who came running from her room.

"Well, it's an accident. She was going up
stairs and she fell."

"You helped her to that accident, you brute!"

"Suppose I did! She was running away, do

you hear? I caught her. I am not sorry that she should know what comes of provoking me. Leave both our doors open, and don't you meddle and take that girl's part, mother, I warn you."

He looked askance, narrowing his eyes, and turned in his hands the hat he had picked up.

"The old nun can go and call the police, and welcome. Let her. The police have not sent those women apart to bring them together again."

"All the same, you've given her a bad beating, Jules," ventured the widow, one of whose eyes was swollen. "She doesn't move."

"The good-for-nothing! She was running away! A woman who has been fed a whole year in this house!"

"But look how white she is!"

"When she has paid me what she owes me, I shall let her go; not before."

"Suppose she shouldn't come to again?"

"Don't give us any sentiment, old mother," he returned, pushing her roughly away. Outside, in the courtyard, in the narrow shadow of his house, he gave orders to the woman, who, suddenly grown "reasonable," made haste to answer to his directions: "Yes, my boy; I shall see to that; I shall take care; I shall go; that shall be done." When he left her, he took care to walk down the hill without hurry, so that he might be seen to be afraid of no one, but to take his own time, and to go where he pleased, more than ever the king of the district. He crossed the bridge over the Cadereau, and entered the town. As soon as his back was turned, all the population

of Montauri ran to his cottage—men, women, and
children, who had all been watching. They had
seen him carrying home Pascale. What had become of her? Had he killed her outright? "I am
going to see," said one. "So am I—make haste,"
called another. And one averred that Prayou was
gone for the police, and one, for a doctor.

They tried to get in by Madame Prayou's door,
but she sent them away; they turned the flank
of the house, therefore, and came by the waste
land behind into Jules Prayou's own abode. They
were excited and angry. Madame Cabeirol, looking like a little Greek fury, was the first, and then
came Madame Lantosque, who still held the wood-
en spoon with which she had been stirring the
soup at home; then Madame Mayol, then two
old women, one of them with a crutch. In the
passage-room there were only a table and a box,
and there at the foot of the stairs lay the motionless figure. The women gathered to look at her.
Some other passion than curiosity was in their
faces.

"Come and see! Do you think she is bleeding?
Yes, there's some blood—I am sure there is.
She has been wounded."

"Better lift her, poor thing."

"Lift her, do you say? Do you mean to say
you pity her?"

"That I do. I think she moved. How white
her hand is—as white as lather."

"Well, then, go and lift her yourself. I won't
touch her. A nun out of her convent—I call it
disgusting."

"I shall not touch her either." "Nor I."
"Nor I." Men were among the speakers.

"She has only got what she deserved."

The shrill voice of Madame Cabeirol screamed:
"She is a horrid woman! And she gave herself
the airs of a lady! When I think that just now
I was helping her with the linen! Well, bleed, my
girl, or die if you like. I know now what you are,
the lowest of the low. Oh, yes, you can hear me.
You are just pretending not to understand, but
you understand well enough. You are a disgrace!"

"A shame to the whole of Montauri," cried a
workman tragically; he had left his luncheon.
And the wretched man, who found it hard to
pay his rent, pushed forward to the foot of the
stair, close to the poor ghastly figure. "You
won't find me handing over money to you again,
you wretch!" he shouted. And, as though the
man's insult had been a signal, all Pascale's
neighbours thronged into the passage. All spoke
at once, some to revile her, some to say merely:
"Leave her alone, don't torment the woman."
Protector, defender, there was none. Some lifted
her arm and let it fall again to see whether she
were conscious; others pushed her with a foot;
others merely stared at her in their contempt.
Jealousies, obscure rancours, human stupidity incapable of withstanding an example, had a part in
this cruelty; but the chief motive at work in the
hearts of these people was doubtless vengeance
for the betrayal of a divine ideal.

The place was still thronged when a voice cried:
"Here's Prayou back again!" It was not so, but

the crowd dissolved. Those who had been tim-
orously compassionate were the last to go, and
they moved away backwards. It was then that
a child came springing up the steps, placed her
hand against the doorpost, thrust a little dark
head within, and peered round towards the foot
of the stair. It was Delphine Cabeirol, to whom
the outcast had spoken in the morning.

"You filthy thing, you!" she cried in her fresh,
childish voice.

Then Pascale lifted her head with difficulty, and
turned her face to the light. The child fled.

Pascale lay back again upon the stair and
wept. Long she wept alone.

The sun that day was declining when some one
cautiously drew near. It was Prayou's mother,
and she was uneasy, and came to look. She
raised the fallen figure, and propped it with her
two hands against the shoulders.

"Come, come, Pascale," she said; "no non-
sense."

But when she met those eyes she was afraid.
She withdrew her hands.

"Don't you want to go to your room?"

The pallid face, stained with blood and tears,
remained rigid. But Pascale looked at the
woman, with the wild and profound look of a
hunted and wounded animal, and her eyes moved,
following the motions of her enemy. The woman
was aware that she had before her something
terrible, a creature brought to despair, on the
yonder side of revolt, no pleader for compassion,
a creature whom extremity of misfortune has

turned into a judge, and who condemns in silence, and has God beyond.

"You don't want me to touch you? As you like. I'm off. You see what you get by going against him. A nice state he has put you into! And he's still in a rage. What did you want to run away for? You—a girl we've kept, who has wanted for nothing."

She took on a coaxing manner.

"Listen to me, now. I'll undertake to speak to him—shall I? I know he's violent, but once it's over, it's over. Come, your old Cousin Prayou will take your part, if you'll just promise not to do it again."

The bleeding lips articulated: "I shall not stay!"

"Where will you go then? Not into the town —you know well enough he has forbidden that."

Pascale struggled to her feet. With her hand against the wall she stumbled to the back door. The woman followed, repeating:

"Where are you going? I want to know where?"

Pascale pointed to the far corner of the waste ground.

"Ah! you are going that way, are you? You have not had enough, I suppose? Do as you like. I'm going in. It's hot enough to kill one out of doors."

But she did not go in until she had seen Pascale stop at the far end of the open space. Pascale went slowly in the stifling heat among the stones and the dusty tufts of dry grass. She held one

hand to her fair hair, at the place where her head
had struck the staircase. She made for the
shade, far from the Prayous' house. There were
old broken walls on that side, holding in the soil
of the nearest olive-grounds. She sat down, with
no purpose or thought except that she would rest
awhile at the end of her chain. All the houses
had closed their doors and windows to the west,
against the late hot sun, and Pascale was feeling
a little relief because there were some fifty yards
between her and these people, all of whom had
made her suffer, when a woman coming from the
city entered the space of waste land. Pascale
knew her. She was the widow Rioul, in her black
dress, with her smooth white hair, her air of dignity
and quiet, and her knitting—the black stockings
always on her needles, the ball of worsted in her
pocket. She stopped close to Pascale, as a neighbour might, for a chat. Pascale, sitting bent over
her knees, did not accost her, but she had to
answer.

"Listen, Madame Pascale, I want to speak to
you."

"It's a long while since you spoke to me at
all. Leave me alone."

"I did not speak because you would not let
me. But I loved you, my child. It was I who
told Sister Justine about you. It was I who
called her. It was I who showed her this morning
the way to Montauri, and who got her away from
the wretched people down by the tank. They
soon let her go when they saw me taking her part.
I saw her safe to the station. I have come with

a message from her. She is at Lyons and she expects you there."

The widow whispered, as though the olive trees could hear her.

"I promised her," she said, "that you would go to-night."

Pascale slowly shook her head, but did not raise it.

"I tried this morning. I am lost, you see, quite lost."

"I know that his friends are everywhere; but I have friends about too. Promise to do what I ask, and I will save you, Madame Pascale."

Gently, seeing that Pascale was listening, she unfolded her plan. She knew in the country near by, beyond the Saint Césaire road on the slope opposite the Puech du Teil, a small proprietor who lived on his farm all the year round. She had given him notice. At night she would take Pascale across the orchards, where they would meet no one, to the farm. Starting from the Nîmes station would be out of the question. Pascale would be hidden and guarded at the farm. She was expected there. Then, at daybreak, Cosse, the farmer, would take her across to the station of Caveirac, or perhaps to some place still more distant.

"At what time will the train be at Caveirac?" asked Pascale.

The widow, happy to find that her plan was accepted, said warmly:

"Thank you, thank you for your confidence. Thank you for being willing to live. How happy

your sisters will be! Listen now to the end;
but I must be quick, for I believe that some one is
watching us, whether Prayou or one of his spies.
As soon as it is dark I shall be at the far end of the
olive orchard, near the Saint Césaire road, on this
side, in the enclosure where hiding is easy; I will
take you through the openings in the orchard
walls. And now you must have a little food."

"In his house?" asked Pascale.

"In his mother's house, yes."

"I shall not go back there."

"Ah! you will go because you will need some
strength; I cannot take you to my own room;
something would be suspected."

"I won't go; I won't go back."

"Madame Pascale, if I ask you to go back and
to eat their bread—as a sacrifice——"

The old woman went on her way, to all appearance absorbed in her knitting. But the words
she had used were such as had once been pow-
erful over the soul of Pascale, and they still had
power.

The evening followed the burning day. The
waste ground was as hot as an oven from which
the red charcoal has just been withdrawn. The
glow was gone from the country. Nothing caught
the light except the stone pines on the high hill,
and they held sheaves of rays from the west.
Pascale stood up.

When she entered the kitchen, Madame Prayou,
surprised, paused in her peeling and slicing of
onions.

"What have you come for?" she asked.

"Give me a towel, I want to wash."

"In here?"

"Yes, in here."

"All right, you can."

"And let me have some bread as well. I have eaten nothing since morning."

"Now you are talking sense. You have come round, I am glad to see."

Pascale said no more. When she had washed away the traces of blood, of tears, and of dust from her face, and had fastened up her hair, shaken loose by the fall, she stood by the window that opened on the road of Montauri, and watched the woman, who was cutting a piece of bread. She loathed that bread. But she said to herself: "I promised, I will keep my word." The mother of Jules Prayou doubtless had some sense of the significance of this daily action, on this one day. She cut the bread and held it at arm's length, and saw that Pascale, having taken it, did not eat it, but held it awhile in her hand. At last, leaning against the window-sill, she raised the bread to her mouth and ate.

The widow looked on; puzzled by the novel kind of submissiveness in her servant, she began a monologue in which protestations of solicitude for the girl's health were mingled with a few adroit questions regarding the work to be done in the house on the morrow, on the following day, ten days later. Pascale heard not a word. She ate, feeling no hunger. She was thinking of the hour when she must go, of the widow Rioul who might turn traitress, of the road, the

meeting-place to be found, of her own battered
body that could hardly stand.

Suddenly her shoulders shrank against the
wall; her eyes wore again their look of terror.
Some one was coming up the street, and her impulse was to hide. But by effort of will she remained at the window, and ate what bread was
left, so that Prayou might see her eat it.

He saw her, with the silent smile of a man who
never doubted of success, but whose success had
been unexpectedly complete. He did not speak
to Pascale; but, seeing his mother busy over the
supper, he said to her:

"Don't expect me this evening, mother. There's
a bull-fight at Arles to-morrow, and I am off to-
night with two friends of mine——"

With his orator's or actor's gesture he swept
his hand towards the foot of the hill, where loitered
a couple of men. Pascale looked straight before
her, but she felt, she felt Jules Prayou's hatred
heavy upon her.

"That's right, my boy," said the mother.
"Good-bye till to-morrow night. I shall take
care of Pascale."

The man went out.

It was then that Pascale looked at him. She
followed him with her eyes. She noticed that he
had his every-day clothes, the blue suit, old and
stained, that he had worn in the morning.

From her place the widow had not ceased to
watch Pascale. Seeing her quiet, seeing her eyes
upon the man as he went, she thought: "I
was a fool to be anxious. She has eaten our

bread in his presence. There will be no more trouble."

She was wrong. Pascale's voluntary humiliation had begun the work of her deliverance.

Slowly came the darkness. Fragments of the rays of day, the smouldering of light, filled the evening air. The smallest details of the distant houses of Montauri were still visible, for the equal light came from all quarters of an untroubled sky; and the world was full of witnesses. People were out in the gardens. All along the street there were voices, and those of women and children pierced the still evening, arrow-sharp. The men were drinking in the wine-shops. Farther off, on the side where stood the slaughter-houses, sounded intermittently the flute of a butcher boy who was practising for a public ball; the harlots of the town were to dance to his music at night.

Towards nine o'clock Pascale leaned out again. She saw the olive trees, in spite of the transparence of the night, massed together in the dusk, like smoke or rolling clouds.

"I am going to bed," she said, and rose.

The widow, dozing, roused herself and replied: "Yes, be quick; you should have gone before."

Pascale began, involuntarily, to walk with a stealthy silence. She crossed the courtyard, hid herself for a few moments in the passage, then opened the back door and stood alone, afraid of what she was about to do, in the pearly night that covered the hill. The way across the waste was all unsheltered. She skirted it, keeping by the garden walls, and when she reached the upper end,

across which ran a terrace, she climbed it by means
of broken stones, and stood among the trees.
Hiding for a moment behind a stem she looked
back and saw that she had not been followed.
Profoundly peaceful was the summer night; the
butcher's little flute had ceased; the sky was thick
with stars. Pascale went up by a row of trees,
then turned to her left. The whole olive country
before her looked like a vague blue sea set with
innumerable islands. And from island to island
went Pascale, crossing quickly, as quickly as
she could in her weakness, shaping her course
towards the orchard corner where the widow
Rioul was to await her. She reached an enclosing wall, and here, afraid to call, afraid of the
sound of her feet among dry leaves, she paused,
she went to and fro in search of an outlet. At
last she found a foothold on the branch of a
dead tree, raised herself, looked over, and there,
straight and thin as the figure of a saint in a church,
stood the widow among the trees.

"Come quick," said the woman. "Thirty steps
or so to your right you will find a way through."

When Pascale had grasped her friend's hand
she grew braver. Together they made their
way across the wide orchard down hill, and then
across another, up hill, and stood on the crest of
the second wave of the billowing country. Here
they came upon the cross-roads. The old high
road to Saint Césaire was divided at this point
by the wedge of a thick wood, and thence formed
two curving ways sweeping apart, widely diver-
gent. The wood was enclosed by walls, and at

the point of the wedge stood two black cypresses, the only tall trees on the whole hill-top; they alone pierced the stars. It was a solitary place, for the little houses—the orchard cottages peculiar to the neighbourhood, the *mazets*—were never inhabited except on Sundays. The widow, finding the breach she knew of in the orchard wall, put her head cautiously through, and listened. Then she returned to fetch Pascale.

"There is no danger," she said. "You have nothing more to fear, you are saved. The farm is close by."

Nothing stirred as they turned the corner where stood the cypresses, and took a steep path leading them to a gate of rusty iron bars, by which hung the handle of a bell.

"We must not ring," said the widow, "I can get in." She unfastened the gate and pushed it open. Pascale found herself in an enclosure, with olive trees in the foreground, and further down a pasture that reached to the bottom of the little valley. Opposite rose the hill called the Puech du Teil. The farmhouse was at hand, and the widow knocked at its door. There was no reply; but soon the two women standing close together could hear a sour voice chiding in *patois:*

"Promised, have you? Then you had no business to promise. You ought to have told me. I don't want a woman of that kind in my house. Not to speak of the danger."

"Be quiet, Louise," replied a man, "I am not going to leave our old friend standing outside; nor the other, either."

A dragging footstep came to the door; the bolt was drawn, and an old, bent man with a fine face baked and rebaked by seventy southern summers drew back to let the women pass in. They paused on the threshold.

"Go in, Madame Pascale," said the widow: "I am leaving you with good people."

"Leaving me?" faltered Pascale.

"I must."

"I beg you, I beg you to stay with me. Oh, the night will be so long! I am afraid, I am dreadfully afraid!"

Pascale put her arms about the neck of this one friend, the only creature who had loved her in the time now at last at an end. "Stay with me. You can go back to-morrow, when we leave."

But she heard the quiet voice in her ear: "It is for your sake I am going back. There would be too much wondering at my absence all night. Something might be suspected. Let me go; do this—it is one more sacrifice——"

The two women kissed each other. Pascale went in alone. The door was closed and the bolt was shot.

"Compose yourself, Madame Pascale," said the old man. "Why, you are as white as a ghost. There's nothing to be afraid of. You're among friends. Among friends, isn't she, Louise? And in the morning, by the first light, we'll be off together to the station at Caveirac."

Pascale had walked into the middle of a wide hall lighted by a small petroleum lamp at the further end on the chimney-piece. A few chairs,

a table, and an old cupboard were all the furniture.
Working clothes hung on the walls, with tools,
whips, and harness.

"As long as a woman isn't married," said the
old man, "she's got a right to run away; that's
how I look at it. You sit down and make yourself
comfortable. A little glass of *carthagène* would
do you no harm. Will you have one?"

But Pascale walked no further. She was
aware of the anger and contempt of a woman
seated by the fireplace, out of the circle of lamp
light. Louise, much younger than her husband,
had hard black eyes, and they wore a look that
bade the stranger begone. Yet she had not
spoken. Cosse, much embarrassed, went on with
his monologue, set chairs, opened the cupboard,
and fumbled inside. There was a clatter of
glasses. He went to the table. "We are good
people, Madame Pascale, good people, who are
not going to leave you in trouble. There's a
right and there's a wrong, that's how I look at it.
I say, Louise, where have you put——"

He stopped, startled.

Some one had lifted the latch and had driven
hard against the door. The bolt held. The
farmer and his wife stood close together; Pascale
listened, ceasing to breathe. So suddenly deep
was the silence that the cigalas were audible,
chirping in the night.

"He is there," then said Pascale. "My poor
people, it's all over."

The door was shaken a second time with
violence, and the voice of Prayou called, "Open,

old Cosse, or I shall batter it in. Pascale is in your house."

"Don't go," breathed the farmer's wife; "don't go, Cosse; don't go and get yourself killed on her account. He doesn't want you, he wants her." And to Pascale she said, "Go, then, go; why don't you go?"

Pascale was shrunk, she looked quite small; her eyes, her whole soul, were on the door—the door upon which her fate was knocking.

"Coming, coming," cried the old man.

He put aside his wife's detaining hands, he hobbled to the wall on which hung the tools and harness. Pascale followed him with her eyes. A storm was within her. The instinctive love of life strove there, and her youth, and her strength, though it had failed under so much agony. The old man went before her. He grasped from the wall the handle of a pick-axe, but he had not yet freed it from the pile of clothes hanging from the same hook, when Pascale stopped him.

"Leave it alone, I am going. He would hurt you," she said.

"And what about you?"

She answered: "He can do me no more harm —no more harm now."

"Are you going to open that door?" asked the voice.

The old man made another effort to go forward, but Pascale barred the way. Standing before him she made her resolution known.

"God orders me to go in your place. I have

sinned against Him, and now He is going to forgive me."

Next she was running to the door, and as she ran she threw over her head, unconsciously preparing for the night air outside, the shawl she had carried on her arm. She undid the bolt. The couple within saw a square of glimmering blue night; they saw a man seizing Pascale and hauling her out; then the square of blue again, the night, their olive trees. And they heard the feet of Prayou and of Pascale hurrying up the path. The man had seized her by the waist. She struggled; at moments she lost her footing, at moments he carried her. So they came to the iron-barred gate. There he relaxed his grip.

"Now let us have it out, *Sister!* and take care— take care of your skin!"

She turned on the path and ran.

"What, again!" he cried.

She had no strength but the strength of terror. She ran up the narrow path leading to the high road, and the stones rolled and gave way under her feet, and brambles caught her gown. One only hope she had—to reach the place where the road divided; there might chance to be passers-by. And she felt by some instinct that the man would stab her less readily if she kept the left of the path, somewhat out of the easiest reach of his right hand. He ran, trotting without effort or hurry, keeping up with the girl who strained and stumbled as she fled. Twice he overtook her, lifting his hand as though the stroke would be then. But he held that murderous hand; he saw

that she still had a little breath, and he knew that
she still could scream.   He let her run.

"Will you come home with me?"

"Never, never!"

"Will you come home?   If you won't I shall
kill you."

The second time he waited for no reply. She
knew that he was feeling in his pocket.   She knew
then, she knew that she was lost, and she could
not scream. They were now near the top of
the hill, and the road lay across their path.
With a last effort Pascale reached the crest and
the two cypresses, and looked, looked in vain for
a figure of man or woman in sight. There was
none. Prayou had let her gain a little distance
in advance of him, and now she heard him behind
her running at last in earnest.   He was coming
up, and coming up on the left.   Before he reached
her she sobbed.   Raising her hands over the distant city, she whispered her last broken words:

"*Miserere mei, Deus.*"

Between her shoulders the knife struck and
pierced her through, pierced her to the breast.

Carried down by the violence of the stroke, the
body rolled to the orchard wall, to the place where
the road turned downhill towards Nîmes, and
near to the little wood that split the way.

Prayou leapt, wrenched out the knife, let fall
the head with the eyes still rolling in their sockets,
ran on the road that followed the line of the hill-
summit, vaulted over a wall, sprang from terrace
to terrace down the slope, and vanished into the
solitary country beyond.

Pascale was already dead. She lay on her back, with the rush of her blood beneath her. It flowed into the furrows made by old storms and floods in the now dry soil. No longer smooth was your tender mouth, poor girl; your golden eyes saw not through the pupils that were wide towards the innumerable stars. The shawl of white wool, drawn over those brows and one pale cheek, had some semblance of the veil. The two cypresses kept watch like tapers in a sanctuary.

At break of day a milkman's cart, coming from the country, reached the summit of the hill. The horse, aware of the scent of death, shied and turned; a boy leapt out on the road to catch the reins. It was then that he saw the body of Pascale.

At the same moment there was a cry, for his sister, now also afoot, was running to the place where lay the dead. Together they raised the shoulders from the ground, and then they saw the blood, and it was fresh.

"Don't touch her, because of the police," said the young man. "No one must touch a body before they come. I'll fetch them. Stay you here, Marie, and keep guard."

It was four o'clock. The girl sat by the murdered head; she was afraid. There was a morning cold in the air. At short intervals she rose, fancying that she heard steps behind the walls. Then she composed herself and thought of the young dead, and looked with pity upon that pallid face. This girl was of her own age; she knew nothing of the stranger, except only her misfortune. She looked at the face and at the hair, of a colour so rare and so beautiful, and her compassion grew, and a tender friendliness crept into her heart. Of old many had felt the same for the living Pascale.

As time went on, the girl on her watch brought forth her rosary. "I don't know," she thought, "whether this poor thing was of my religion or not; and she may very likely have been a woman of the town. It does not matter now; I will pray for her."

The early broad flood of day opened upon the hill of Montauri and upon the long succession of its neighbour hills. It touched the hands, the chin, the cheek of Pascale. But the fair eyelashes moved not, and the open eyes were glassy towards the sky from which the stars were gone.

At about that time the *procureur* of the Republic, having received notice from the mayor's office, whither the milkman had first betaken himself, hastened to the cab-stand on the boulevard Amiral Courbet, and gave orders that he should be driven "to the scene of the crime." Agents of police, the commissary, and a doctor were already on the road. And in that carriage the body of Pascale was brought to Nîmes. It was received at the hospital on the Montpellier road, the place where Pascale in former years had spoken of her own sensitiveness: "I cannot bear to look at a wound or even to hear about it." The gates were opened wide. The carriage stopped, and two men bore the body between them beyond the principal building into a low amphitheatre that served as a dissecting-room.

The news of the murder had now roused the city. The magistrates had drawn up the warrants against the fugitive. Information was at hand—it abounded and superabounded. The inhabitants of the western district were ready to tell all they knew to the journalists, the police, the porters at the hospital: "I knew her; so did I, and I; she was a near neighbour," and so forth.

During the afternoon all the dwellers at Montauri had passed through the large hall in which Pascalc now lay; many had wept, many had knelt; all had felt the pity of the living for the past sorrows of the dead; and some had reproached themselves in silence for their insults against one in grief; she was in grief no more, but she could no longer forgive them. Two women, one leaning on the other, entered that death chamber—the widow Rioul and Sister Justine. The old Superior, summoned by telegram, had come from Lyons, and on the way from the station she had hardly heard the story told by her friend. "My child is dead," she wept; "my little girl, my Pascale!" She saw nothing, nor did she hear the shop-keepers at their doors, who said: "Look, do you remember? That is the Mother, the nun!" She opened her arms at the door, as she had opened them not many hours before to the lost one, and then she turned, she faltered, she hid her face against the charitable breast at her side. Before them lay the body of Pascale, stretched upon one of three sloping tables. A sheet was spread upon it up to the breast, leaving uncovered the neck that had been so slender and smooth, and was now livid and falling into hollows like sand when the sea has ebbed. The hair was scattered. And there was no taper near, no flower, not a spray of the box blessed with holy water that is put about the dead; not a sign that any creature had ever loved Pascale. Only, at the head of the room was the sign of our common hope, the image of Christ upon His cross. And above the head of the table where she lay, a large black-board, placed there long ago, bore the inscription: "We have been what you are; and what we are now, you, too, shall be."

The poor maternal heart felt such a pang that Justine for a moment could not look. But, gathering her courage again, she went up to the hard bed of her child, and on the frozen forehead laid the kiss of peace. Then she knelt at the head, and the widow knelt at the feet. There was no sound except that of the attendants walking impatiently outside, waiting, because closing time had come.

When Sister Justine rose to her feet, she searched in her pocket and drew thence the large rosary, the sacred rosary that hangs at the girdle of a nun. She joined Pascale's hands, she bound them together with the chain of beads, the "Our Father" and "Hail Mary" of so many prayers.

"Sister! what are you doing?" whispered the widow. "Not your rosary—surely you do not mean——"

"She lost hers," answered Justine. And she

folded the little fingers of Pascale into the position
so familiar to them in the days of her purity.
Pascale fingered the beads as though she prayed
again.

When this was done, Justine stood awhile, and
her eyes lingered on the face she should see no
more.

"You are like the world," she said to her
friend, "you are hard. But I know that half of
her sin does not lie with her, but with those who
drove her from my arms. I know that what
share was hers she expiated, and that she voluntarily accepted death. My child returned to God
when she heard me speak the name of Edwige."

*　　　*　　　*　　　*　　　*　　　*

Two days more did Sister Justine remain in
the town, sent from administration to administration, from the police to the prefect and from
the prefect to the mayor, all in authority in the
disposal of the dead. She pleaded passionately
for her desire; a few of the citizens were interested in her efforts and helped her. Finally she
gained her cause. She had leave to take her
child to the old cemetery of the weavers of
Saint Irénée, where lay the Mouvands of the
Croix Rousse.

On the evening of the fourth day the gates
of the burial ground of Loyasse were opened for
the passing in of the hearse of the poor. It went
down beyond the end of the sycamore avenue, to
the place where the graves are close together,
about a small fort, long disused, whence can be

seen so many hills and so many villages upon their slopes. It was still light. Four women followed Pascale to her grave. For one day they had clothed themselves again in the dress and the veil of their vows. They had gathered in haste from the utmost ends of France, and on the morrow they would be gone thither again. They were Sister Justine, Sister Danielle, Sister Edwige, and Sister Léonide. The silk merchant's little treasure, the legacy left to their indigence, had bought the ground, had bought the cross hard by, had paid for the journey of the mourners, and no more. Absolute poverty, the poverty that means perpetual separation, was before them all. They knew it, but their thoughts were not for themselves. Elect souls, their thoughts were thoughts of love. Of her they thought, for her they prayed, whose face, whose eyes, whose tenderness, whose appeal, were never to pass from their memories on earth.

And they prayed for the children of their old school, scattered now, and assuredly loved no more as they had once been loved; for their old district and its well-remembered poor, its weak ones, its angry ones, its unhappy ones, for all the sufferings that it was so keen a suffering to be cut off from helping. And they prayed for those who, willing all the evil or not, whether cruel, or only ignorant of heavenly and divine and charitable things, had brought about disaster and had reached their ends.

The priest finished his service and withdrew, the grave-diggers lowered the coffin, and the earth was cast upon her who had been Pascale. The Sisters lingered. Once again they were "in community," and thus in obedience they awaited orders. It was only at the word of the Superior that they took leave of the grave and of Loyasse. They might then be seen, close together, on the road to Saint Irénée, a little huddled group; they talked fast, trying to say many things in the brief time that was theirs. And the joy of being again together overflowed in spite of the restraining pain.

On the hill they paused to look once more on the huge city before them; then, at the corner of a solitary lane, they kissed each other, without tears, for this grief was only for themselves, and went their divided ways: two ways, then three, then four. They drew apart and passed into the crowd, and offered to God, on behalf of their dead Pascale, the pang of another and a final parting.

THE END.